I0580711

VOICELESS

A VOICE UNHEARD & FINALLY TOLD

The Autobiography

Lisa Ward & Olivia Tishaee

VOICELESS

A Voice Unheard & Finally Told

By Lisa Ward & Olivia Tishaee

Front and Back cover images by Frame of Elegance

Photography by Michael Robbins

Graphic design by Guillermo Quirindongo.

Edited by FaLessia Booker, The Editing Expert.

Book set up: Jazzy Kitty Publications

Printed by Humble Doc Publishing in the United States of America.

ISBN: 978-1-7330302-3-6

Library of Congress Control Number: 2024913990

To Our Readers

hrough Voiceless, Olivia, and Lisa are on a mission to give those who are silent a voice. Many people have been told their words do not matter.

Various individuals are encouraged to be seen but should dare not be heard, turning their truths into a lie. When pain is ignored, many individuals part with reality just to function on a day-to-day basis.

To the Voiceless, you are more than silent, mute, or unheard. Never feel that your words are invaluable because they are beyond priceless. The era of being seen and not heard is over. You have the right to release all baggage, all stress, all fear, and all guilt; you are not at fault. Allow us to use our voices and our stories to help you open the door to cancel all generational curses. You will be forever grateful to the new, free, and outspoken you. We now grant you a voice that is more than heard; it will be finally acknowledged.

Sincerely Yours,

Lisa Ward & Olivia Tishaee

ACKNOWLEDGEMENTS

Lisa Ward:

First, I must thank my Savior, Jesus Christ, for giving me the strength to complete this assignment. I am blessed to be chosen to do three books that could change the future generation. I want to thank everyone who has touched my life in one way or another.

I must give a big thank you to my manager Dr. Tamica Potts who believes in me and all the things I want to do. I thank you for seeing things in me I might not see in myself. Thank you for all the hard work and, long hours that you put into my career. Thank you for helping me be a better businesswoman, owner, and founder.

I also want to give my business manager/sister Frances a big thank you for always supporting me in everything I do. Most of all with this book particularly. She is my rock for so many reasons. She is also the reason I stay grounded, and I wouldn't be the woman I am today if it wasn't for her standing by my side.

I never thought I could be the author of multiple books as well as my autobiography, so I must thank my family and friends, who always encourage me to never give up on me.

Thanks also goes out to my sisters, Mary AKA Divine Beauti & CEO Felita, we are not able to see or talk every day, but our sisterhood and love is unbreakable. I know that our sisterhood is even stronger after the 2023 Christmas.

To my children, grandchildren, godchildren, nieces, nephews, brothers, mother, and to my unconditional love of my life, I do this for you. You are the reason I keep pushing to be all I can be.

To Olivia, we did it again, but this time even bigger and better. God brought us together to complete an assignment bigger than either one of us ever could imagine. I know and understand why with each project he gives us. I could not have done the double autobiography with anyone else because our journey was already written for us to do. I thank you for giving me the strength and courage to walk in my truth and help others do the same. I also thank you for trusting me overall.

KIP SHU, my fashion stylist and friend, thank you for always making me look good and helping me with my dreams. To Amanda and Alina, thank you for standing by me. To Jamil Bey, thank you for being there for me. Helping when needed. Being that supportive person and dropping things just to make sure we get to where we need to be. Thank you for being a protective person even when I am OK.

To my team, there are no words for all you have done for me and with me. Also, I want to give a deep and special thank you to, Robin Brown, Terrance Genwright, Bertha Stone, Amori, Françoise Campbell, Robert J Moore, Councilwoman Dr. Corrine Upshur, Kevin "Sugar Daddy" Woodley, C J Meenan, Ulysses Carter, Hayley Mercado, Taniah Delina, Shelly Shell Williams, Representative Sherry Dorsey Walker, Kenneth Koon, Alexis Spight, Pastor Al "Iz-Real" Motley, Kimani Jackson, Michael Robbins, G. Jurel Jones, Randy McMillian, Shayla Parries, Guillermo Quirindongo, Malliki Saddler (AKA DJ Kaotic), Red Spade, Ira Spencer, Latoya Brat-Richards, Teasa Jefferson, and My Godsister Mo Johnson who I love to the end of the earth.

To Michael Robbins, owner of Frame of Elegance Photography: Thank you so much for being by our side every step of the way. We ask and you always support us; you bless us with your wisdom. Thank you so much for everything you do. You make us look good in the public's eyes. I appreciate you very much. Thank you for being the photographer for the *Voiceless* and *EBD* projects. God bless you!

To Tierra Johnson and 2Shot Visuals, I want to thank you for jumping right into helping us with my artists. You're a blessing to the movement and we appreciate you. We will never forget you for being there for us!

Olivia Tishaee:

First and foremost, I would like to thank my Lord and Savior, Jesus Christ; without Him, I would not be here to see this moment.

I would like to thank my mother; without the life-changing decision that she made, I would not have a story to tell. I would like to thank my sister Gail who has always been my support person, no matter what. We are like Celie and Nettie; no one can come in between our bond.

To my brother Corey, who always said, "Sis, you must write your story. You have to dream big." Well, this is just the beginning, Bro.

Thank you to my grandma Bernie (RIP) for the talks on life. I understand now.

My circle is very small, and I want to thank the ladies of my life. Bintu, my sister from another mother; she is my lifeline and I love you dearly. I know I have been crazy busy but know you and the kids are always in my heart.

Nicole (my Chica), my firecracker, you have been and always will be my ride or die. I am the calm to your storm. Love you, my Chica. We can go months without talking and we don't need to talk every day, but when we do get together, or talk it's like we have never missed any time. The love I have for you is unmatched.

Poppa Charles, thank you for stepping into a place in my life that my real father had never even thought of. (Hell, my real father does not even know I am alive). Orin Charles did not think twice when it came to inviting me into the family. Because of him, I now know what it looks like to be a daddy's girl. Not only am I now a poppa's girl, but I gained two successful brothers Jermaine and Andre. who are so easy to fall in love with. Through the two of them, I gained two sisters-in-law, Robyn and Lauren. I can't thank you all enough for opening your hearts to me. I know I said this in my first book, but I want you to understand just how much you all mean to Alex and me.

To Councilwoman Dr. Corrine Upshur and Representive Sherry Dorsey Walker, thank you for your utmost love and support. Thank you for being the ladies that you are and believing in our journey. Tameka Potts, I know I am always M.I.A., but your love alone for me is more than you know. There will never be enough thanks that I can give you, but in this moment, I am trying, but it is not working…LOL! Continue being your authentic self. It's what makes you great at what you do.

Lisa Ward, thank you for sharing this journey of telling your story. I can truly say that without you, I would not have done this. I still don't like you, but here we are making our mark on the world. Blessings and continued success to you!

Lastly, I would like to thank my three permitted heartbeats Damisi, Marquan, and Alexandra for always saying, "Mom, whatever makes you happy." Damisi, you and I have grown up together and I love our bond. You were my first true love to show me what unconditional love really is. Thank you for walking this journey with me. Marquan, you and I are so much alike we clash. You have taught me a lot. You, my child, have made me strong in a way I did not know I needed to be strong. For that, I love you so much. Alex, my surprise child—you stormed into this world and when I say I have enjoyed every moment I can't tell you how much. Continue being who you are—a strong, beautiful, very intelligent young lady. The way you see life and grab it by the balls is what it takes to conquer what is needed in life. Remember who you are and whose you are (8/4). To all my kids, I love you more than you will ever know. To my grandkids, you have made me fall in love all over again. To my Aiden (so big!) you, my baby, are loved to infinity and beyond. You are the reason my heart melts. To my granddaughters, you are going to take this world by storm, and I can't wait to witness it!

Who I Was and Now Who I Am Becoming

I, who was formerly known as Tishaee Olivia, wanted people to be careful with me. I would only act like I was indestructible. When you've gone through the trauma I have, you learn how not to grieve or to grieve quickly. There was never a time to just break. The world never slowed down for my personal suffering and intake. I was too young to understand how to heal. My arms weren't strong enough to hold myself together. It was impossible to know which pieces were meant to come with me and which ones were meant to be left behind. Who to walk away from and whom it's safe to turn towards. So, I carried all the heaviest ones I could. People believe me to be insensitive, but that would be far from the truth; I feel everything—too many wrong things, for the most part. I am learning to let my successes overshadow my mistakes. The love in my life has always outweighed all the heartache. Even though I've carried the heaviest pieces with me all this time, many of them were never mine to carry. Please be careful with me. You are getting a side of me I rarely show. A side I'm only now getting familiar with. A side that will no longer be VOICELESS. J. Raymond, you have captured me with this piece. Thank you for helping me express what I had not been able to do on my own.

The New and Improved

Olivia Tishaee

TABLE OF CONTENTS

Introduction i

Chapter 1: Life in the Beginning..1

Chapter 2: Unfamiliar Territory..10

Chapter 3: Unveiling the Unknown..15

Chapter 4: The Dungeon..24

Chapter 5: Dyslexic at the Kitchen Table...28

Chapter 6: Graduation..32

Chapter 7: My First and Only Male Love...36

Chapter 8: Hatred For Your Child..42

Chapter 9: The Rape of My Soul..48

Chapter 10: Watching...60

Chapter 11: No Justice, No Peace..64

Chapter 12: Court Time..72

Chapter 13: Connecting the Dots...77

Chapter 14: Reunited With the Real..83

Chapter 15: The Kidnapping...87

Chapter 16: Street Life (Off Track A Bit)..90

Chapter 17: The Dirty Thirties...97

Chapter 18: Music, Money, and Manipulation 101

Chapter 19: LGBT...108

Chapter 20: A Voice Unheard & Finally Told...............................115

Survivor Resources...117

About the Authors..118

Sponsorship..120

INTRODUCTION

"God doesn't make mistakes."

Olivia and I came together because when we were born, God had a journey for us that we didn't see or ever understand what was taking place. When someone is facing the type of horrible disadvantages that we had to face as children, teens, and young adults, many people wonder how they survived. At the time we didn't know ourselves. We just took the life we were given one day at a time. We probably didn't see it as living; we only saw it as surviving as long as we could. To survive meant to be silent about what was happening to us.

If we broke the silence, then that meant other people we cared about could also be hurt the same way we were—or worse. We were forced to make hard adult decisions as children if we wanted to even see tomorrow. The transparency that we put into this book was so you can truly understand the pain that we endured. We did it this way for those who have no idea what it is like to go through the things that we have shared with you in this book. There is a big difference when you can envision the person's actual pain. You might have a better understanding now, you're not able to be of help if you really can't understand the pain that person is feeling. Olivia and I don't have to go deep with our conversation because we already understand the circumstances. People need to know that humans didn't survive by being the strongest in the jungle. Humans survived by the ability to think. Olivia and I learned that the true power in surviving was our minds. As we got older, we learned that the greatest thing we can do is use our journey and gift as a tool to help others. God is who truly prepares you without you even noticing that He is doing it.

Today, Olivia and I might not have had a normal upbringing like normal kids should have. Our young life was preparing us for the assignment that God had for us today, years later. That assignment is to help others understand that they are not alone, and they do not have to endure the silence anymore. That is why God assigned us to do the *Voiceless* book and documentary to show you all the things that happen if you stay silent. Our stories will show you the consequences that come with that. We must stop turning our heads and sweeping things under the rug. All it is doing is creating broken adults and keeping the pain going on for generations to come. With our book, we not only want to show you the bad but also show you that you can survive and come out on top. The things that we must endure that are disadvantages are really advantages for someone to use later in life. I know it's hard to believe that but just look at Olivia and me. We are no longer silent because we are going to make a difference in this thing we call life. We are no longer the "Voice Unheard." "We Are The Voice That Is Finally Told." So, we are asking you to join us in the VOICELESS MOVEMENT by supporting the book, the merchandise, and the documentary so we can help others like us.!!!!!!!! We hope that the *Voiceless* book truly helps you get back your power.

CHAPTER 1

Life in the Beginning

Tishaee

My mother was always soft-spoken. I don't ever recall her raising her voice once. We used to live in a one-bedroom apartment in Stockton Station. At that time, it was my mother, my new baby brother, and myself. I used to softly pinch him so I could hear him cry because he had the cutest cry in the entire world and of course so I could hold him before my mom came to his aid.

As you continue to read, you will learn more about my family and me. I want you to understand I would do anything to protect them, even if it meant I would be the one hurting daily. That is what a big sister's job is in my eyes anyway. There were things that made me happy from time to time. I enjoyed going outside and playing with the neighborhood kids. I would stay out there all day until I had to be dragged inside. One summer day, I was outside playing a game to see where the rocks land; my right eye found out quickly, and man did that hurt! My mom was gentle when it came to making sure I was okay, and I felt safe until maybe every other night around midnight. I only remember the time because my mom had a clock that had big red digital numbers and I knew how to count early in age due to my mother being a schoolteacher.

I have heard many stories about why my mom did not keep her children. I was told someone dropped something into her drink and she has not been mentally right since. I also heard that after each kid she gave birth to, her mind slipped back into time. Back then, it was called a nervous breakdown.

Another story was that she was lied on, and Social Services took us from her; another was that she had an opportunity to keep us in the family, but she denied my grandmother the right to take us in and become our legal guardian. Now this is beyond being selfish and just thinking of yourself. That is how I felt once I found out what she had done. During that time, there was no such thing as grandparents having rights so even though my grandmother (may she rest in peace) fought for us, my mom still had the final say.

As far as I am concerned, my mom is the reason behind everything that happened to me. Whatever the true reasoning is, I will never really know. Back to the matter at hand, there was this guy who would visit Mom like clockwork on certain nights. He never came around during the day; it was always at night so I never saw who he was; I just remembered his voice; I could describe it in a line-up if I had to. His tone was always very harsh (or maybe that was his everyday tone). It was deep, almost like the late singer Barry White. One night, he came over and I was not quite asleep. He and my mom were in the bedroom at the time. I sat up and in a very nasty tone, he told me to lay back down. My mom never intervened in the mysterious man correcting me as he and my mom left the room. I used to (and still wonder) if he was my dad. I have never been introduced to him and I have never been told who my father was. The man that my mother did say was my father was just a sperm donor. He has denied me more than once, showing me exactly how he felt about me. So, I stopped pushing the issue; if my mom could not give me the answer, why should I expect anyone else to do what she could not?

I can't tell you when we moved into my grandmother's house nor how long we stayed. There isn't much I can say at all, but I remember the layout of the house. What I do know is the family of three people now became four. It was now my new baby sister, my brother, my mother, and myself. According to the family, my baby sister was an identical twin. Unfortunately, the other twin did not make it.

I always knew the location of my grandma's residence in East Camden. I somewhat remember my granddad. He was a very slender, tall, light-skinned man with dark curly hair. I would run to him in the kitchen, and he would sit me on the countertop, and we would eat breakfast. Me just saying this brings a small smile to my face. I was safe and comfortable, and this man loved me, so I guess it's safe to say I was a grandpa's girl. This house was full of love; no one was coming in and out all hours of the night and no one was yelling at me. Then one day, the family just disappeared. I learned fast that we all ended up in the hands of Social Services for a few months or more to a family that was amazing from what I remember.

This family lived in the country in a beautiful home, with a huge front and backyard. I loved playing in the front yard, picking the flowers, and playing in the water holes. We ate dinner together as a family. I would catch the bus to school and this beautiful lady would be at the bus stop every day waiting for my arrival; life was good from a kid's perspective, but that was short-lived.

I know you must be thinking the same thing as I was. Why did they take us from this amazing family that understood what loving children truly meant? "The system" as it was known was notorious for putting children with whomever was willing to get a check and getting the case off their desk. This is exactly what the New Jersey Division of Youth and Family

Services, also known as DYFS, and the court system did with us. Not only did they just drop us off; they said, "Fuck those kids" in my opinion. We were trash and an extra income for people who should never have been allowed to have kids under their roof. With all that being said, we ended up with a family whose name we would keep for a lifetime. Make sure your seatbelts are fastened, because I am about to take you on the ride of your life!

Genesis 1: In the beginning, God created me for this life.

Lisa

I was a kid who was happy and loved her mother with all my heart. I thought my mother was fly and so beautiful. I was just a little confused because, to me, my family did not look like me. I was so light-skinned, and they were so much darker than me that I thought I was White. I didn't care because my mom loved me with all her heart, and I was a daddy's girl. I was told many stories about my childhood that I don't remember, but most of the ones I do are good, and some are bad.

My very first happy memory as a little kid was my amazing great-grandmother who was my best friend. You see, my great-grandmother was like a big kid in my eyes, I could not do anything wrong. I'm not sure what age my great-grandmother was, but I would help feed her and watch TV shows with her and she wouldn't let anyone mess with me or even hit me, no matter what I did as a little girl. Now I don't remember the things I was doing, but I remember hearing my great-grandmother's voice yelling at my mother telling her and my father to 'let her be" and "You better not touch my Piggy." I don't have as many memories as most people would love to have, and I wish I had more of my great-grandmother, but unfortunately, I don't.

Now there is one major event that I thought I would not remember, but it is a memory that is as clear as day. I don't remember how the day started, but I do remember where I was standing. I was in the middle of the living room floor holding my stepmother's hand and looking towards the hallway and the next thing I saw was a man in a black uniform pulling a stretcher out of our hallway with a long black bag on top and another man at the other end pushing. I am not sure why this day is so clear to me. I have no idea what age I was when all this took place. I saw them walk right past me and somehow, I knew my great-grandmother was in that bag, and as I saw them walk out the door, never to see her again was more hurtful and deeper than I could imagine. I cried the whole time I was writing this.

My mom had to leave me for the first time with my father to put my great-grandmother to rest in her hometown. My mom said, "We are going for a ride, Baby. I was excited because I always loved going anywhere with my mom." As we were riding, she said, "Piggy, I have to take Grandmom home and you're going to be with your father and stepmother for a couple of days until I get back. I need you to be a big girl for me."

I don't know who they thought I was at that age, but when I tell you I showed out—that's an understatement. I cried as soon as my mother kissed me and said bye. As my father and I were driving away, I was looking at her out the back window of the car saying, "Mama, don't leave me."

I am not sure how long my mother was out of town, but I got very sick, and I didn't eat or sleep much. My father had to call my mother to see if she could talk to me and get me to eat. My father says to my mother, "This girl will not eat or stop crying! All she is doing is asking for you."

"Well, Mike, put her on the phone, and I will see what I can do." My father calls out to me and says, "Piggy, your mother is on the phone."

I ran to that phone so fast and there was no crying being done as I grabbed it out of my father's hand. "Hello, Mama! When are you coming home? I miss you and I want you to come get me."

My mother tells me, "Baby I'll be home Saturday, so I need you to stop crying and eat your food like your father says and I promise I'll be there soon."

I didn't like my mother's answer and as she was telling me she loved me, I was crying so hard I spit up. The whole time my mother was gone, I did not eat anything and I gave my father a run for his money.

I woke up Saturday morning and he told me, "Piggy you don't have to cry no more. Mama is coming home today and we must go get her."

"Dad, I must look nice for Mama, so you are doing my hair, right? He smiled at me and said, "Yes, come and sit down. We don't have much time."

We pulled up to my auntie's house in the parking lot in the projects. I kept asking my father where Mama was. "I don't see her," I said.

Once he parked, I saw my mama coming out of a car. I jumped out of my father's car yelling, "Mama, Mama!"

He yelled, "Stop Piggy! I don't want you to get hit by any of these cars in the lot."

I didn't listen and kept running until I got to my mother and jumped right into her arms. She looked like she was upset, but understood that I missed her so much that we just held each other until we heard a car horn and a person saying, "Can you please move to the side so we can pass?" But the people in the car had smiles on their faces as they passed, seeing that a little girl was just happy to see her mother.

As we were on our way home, I asked my mother if great grandmama was OK now. She looked at me and said, "Yes babe. She is home with her other family members and with God in Heaven. She is not in pain or sick or need anyone to help her eat or get dressed anymore."

I said, "That is good Mama."

You would think from this that my life was amazing, but as time went by, I was faced with some health issues. My family was worried about me because I stopped eating and I just stayed in bed with my mom when I was not in school. I was taken to the hospital where we found out that I must have surgery immediately to fix a condition that I was born with which my mother never told me about.

The surgery was very painful from what I can remember. I couldn't stand up straight for some time. I started to feel better after a few months. Also, I could finally eat! My weight started to pick up and I am now able to go home. I was very skinny from the time I was born to the age of seven. I never understood why until I became ill. I also wore glasses at the age of four or five years of age. I thought that was crazy young, but I couldn't really see that well.

My mother and I lived in the projects. She didn't really let me do many outside events because it was bad in the neighborhood—at least that is what I thought. Don't get me wrong; it was partly true, but I learned later that there was more to the story.

I was a kid that had two lifestyles— one being from the projects and the other the suburbs. One I liked a lot and the other I loved. One day, I was home playing in the kitchen and this woman came over to see my parents.

As my father opened the door, he said a bad word along with, "Look who the cat drug in. Mama, Maria is here."

She looked at the lady with a look of surprise but still gave her a hug and kiss. The lady said, "Hello Mama."

Now I was only about two or three years old, and I wanted to know why this lady was calling my mother mama. I just kept playing with my little cousin. Mama called to me, "Piggy come here and say hello to Ms. Maria."

"Hello."

She just looked at me as if something was wrong with my dress. She finally said hello and asked Mama, "Can we talk in the back?"

"Now you girls stay right in here till I come and get you for lunch."

We said okay. Ms. Maria came into the kitchen without my mother and watched us playing. I got up to tell my mother I was ready to eat now and ask if we can go to McDonalds.

As I went to walk past, the woman stopped me and said, "You are lucky to be here," and then she slapped me so hard my mother and father heard it and ran into the kitchen. My father grabbed me in his arms to see if I was OK and my mother pushed Maria and told her, "You need to go, but if you ever put your hands on her again, I'll kill you."

I don't remember what happened next, but I do remember what I had on; It was a white and black dress with a touch of red around the waist. I just could not understand why the woman hit me and why she didn't like me. The next thing I knew, as fast as she came, she went just as fast.

God, grant me the serenity to accept the things I cannot change, the courage to change the things I can, and the wisdom to know the difference.

—Reinhold Niebuhr, Lutheran theologian

CHAPTER 2

Unfamiliar Territory

Tishaee

One would think that finally settling into a home and family who wants to keep us all together would be great, but this was just the start of a lifelong nightmare—one I never saw coming. Before the parents adopted us, everything was great: the parents were great, the social workers did their jobs and checked on us like they should have, and we even received visits from our birth family members. For a little while, life was good. My Aunt Lil (may she rest in peace) would come by and bring us all types of gifts and rub us down in Vaseline. We were the shiniest kids in the neighborhood! I was excited to see her—she was always loud and spoke quickly, but she loved us nevertheless. Over time, things changed, and folks stopped coming around to see how we were doing. Meanwhile, the parents started to show their true colors—alcoholism. I had never experienced that before, so this was a scary adjustment for me. However, I adjusted in the best way I knew how at the age of five or six years old. The "loving parents" were not so loving; the real parents were slowly unveiling their true identities. The real parents were known for drinking, screaming, fighting, and arguing.

The best part of this chaos was it stayed just between the parents. I was just subjected to the noise during the nights when you are supposed to be at peace. Again, this was something I was not familiar with, so I had those nights where I would wet the bed because I was too scared to make a sound if I had to go to the bathroom. Their arguing alone was too much for me to handle; my mother never raised her voice at me. Now I am in this strange and new environment and it does not feel good at all, but here we are. Let's make the best of a miserable situation. If this is all they are doing, I can handle this until a familiar face comes by to visit me and when they do, I can let them know that I want to go back home; all I need to do is wait and be patient.

While waiting, I remember getting my first brand-new bike and learning how to ride without training wheels. This was the first of many falls. It took me about a week to get it together; after that, I was one of the few speed demons in the neighborhood. One day. I was riding so fast that I came around a curve too fast, my bike came up from under me, and down I went. I skinned the entire left side of my body. Those scars lasted for a minute, but it did not stop me from going back out there and putting the speed to the pedals.

In the meantime, I was still waiting and waiting and waiting, but as time went on, I realized that no one was coming to check on me, let alone coming to my aid. Hope was slowly fading in my world; my family had truly abandoned me. My thoughts were, *"How could my family not want me or my siblings? Why are they not coming to see about us?"* Then I was told by the parents that my family no longer wanted to come and see me or my siblings. My heart was crushed and the hope I had no longer mattered; this was the new norm for not only me but my brother and sister. So, I was left with never seeing my actual blood relatives ever again, out of sight, out of mind, but I remembered what was important to me: my grandmother's house. I will forever remember both inside and out including the location. Then it happened; the adoption was soon to come.

A year later around the summer of 1985, we were moving from a 2-bedroom townhouse into a 3-bedroom single-family home. I can see the house numbers 1224 in Camden, New Jersey. I was thinking, "Great! Maybe things are changing," and for a while everything was great. My brother had his own bedroom, and my sister and I shared a nice-sized bedroom. There was an unfinished basement, living room, family room, back yard, and a nice kitchen with a one-and-a-half size bathroom. The area in which we lived was nice—it was family-friendly.

Looking at us, we were the perfect family and we ended up with another baby sister from a different family. So now we were a family of six, three girls and one boy. Everything was falling into place; we were all in school or daycare and living our best life.

We were being adopted, so our names changed or were rearranged. Personally, no one could ever pronounce Tishaee (Tee-Shay). I was called everything but my name by adults mainly. I remember being asked if I would like to switch my middle name to my first name. That would make me Olivia Tishaee. I was teased because my name was Olivia, so the kids would call me Olive, Olive Oyl, you name it; I was called it. I hated it so much, but what could I do? My name was now my name. I found out years later that the change was to keep my birth family from finding me. Now we are permanently part of this family and carry their last name. All good—we are now one big happy family going on with our lives.

Life was not always bad—we had tons of food, we played outside, had bikes, skates, games systems, and whatever the last gig or clothes that were out, we had it. The neighborhood kids stayed visiting at our front door. When it came to being outside, we were normal kids. Double Dutch was my thing and playing jacks; 1,2,3, red light, and hide and go seek. We were allowed to be kids when the parents were sober. There was a park across the street from where we lived in "pollock town" that had a huge water tower in the middle of the park. I was curious to know if there was a cover on top of the tower, so one day, a few of us went to the park and the kids helped me reach the ladder so I could climb up. I got more than halfway up the tower, my shoelace got caught, and I slipped and fell backward on the ladder. My friends were panicking and did not know what to do, but I knew if I fell to the ground, I was as good as dead. Thank God I did not fall! I was hanging upside down and my foot had intertwined in the ladder. As they were screaming for help, I was telling them to shut the hell up because if the parents found out I was sure to get my ass whipped. So, I used all my upper body strength and was able to pull myself upright and once that was done, I climbed my little body down fast and jumped in my friends' hands, caught my breath, and ran home to regroup. This was never spoken of for at least three years.

So, life did not always have bad memories. We were kids and did normal kid stuff. We lived in the corner store—BBQ corn chips, Snickers, and a Hi-C fruit punch was my favorite. I walked to school with my friends. I talked on the phone, and I recorded music on tape cassettes (for those who remember what tape cassettes are LOL). I wore MC Hammer pants (who hasn't?), and the British Knights better known as BK's. I would go to the school dances which were called sock hops, Uh-oh…I think I am starting to tell my real age! We spoke into the fans to change our voices and let me not forget about Chinese rope and the neighborhood house parties. Yes, there were some good times, but the bad unfortunately outweighs the good.

But Jacob said, "Sell me your birthright as of this day." Genesis 25:31, NKJV.

However, my birthright was not sold, but stolen. I would have never given my family up!

CHAPTER 3

Unveiling the Unknown

Lisa

I remember a nice sunny day when I was about six years old. My mother didn't let me go outside like other kids and play. I never really understood, but at the time it was OK. However, she would do all types of things to make the days fun. My father was not living with us then; he and my stepmother had a home in the suburbs. I liked going to their house on the weekends. It was me and my mother/grandmother for the most part. On this day, I was home sick from school for about a week. (I was sick a lot when I was younger). I remember one day I was feeling much better, so my mother wanted to teach me how to turn Double Dutch and hula hoop because I was not good at it. In the middle of us playing and doing the hula hoop and for those who might not remember or know what that is. It's a big ring that you put over your head and around your waist to make it go round and round without stopping or messing up. You also didn't want it to hit the floor because you would need to start all over again.

"Hey, Baby. Come sit with me," asks my mother/grandmother, "I have something to talk to you about."

"Ok, Mama. What is it?"

"I need you to know I love you very much and what I am about to tell you does not change anything about us. You understand what I am saying?"

"I think so. What is it that you must tell me? Are you OK? You're not going away again, right?"

"No Baby, I'm not going anywhere. So, this might be hard for you to hear and most of all understand. I am not your birth mother.”

“What do you mean you are not my mother?”

“No, I am your guardian, and you were appointed to me by the courts, which I requested. You see, your mother was not from here and she had nowhere to go or live. So, me and your father took her in off the street. She was not always emotionally happy with her life and would just take off for no reason. I asked her one day why she would just pick up and leave. She said there is a feeling that comes over her and she just must go, no matter what is going on with her. When she left this time, she came back pregnant with you, and she stayed with us the whole time until you were born. After you were born, she left two days later, and we didn’t see her until that day you saw her and she put her hands on you.”

That was my mother.

“So let me understand. She comes back here, sees me, and never tells me who she really is. Then she hits me and goes away after you stop her from hitting me again.”

“Yes, Baby. I know this is a lot and like I told you, I will never let her take you away from me, but I need you to understand that she is your mother and you must respect her if she does come back around.”

“Respect her? For what? She left me, she hit me and told me I should be happy that you’re my mother. What mother would do that or even tell a child something like that?”

“She is not OK emotionally. You just have to forgive her and live the best life that you can. You must also look at it this way—she could have put you in the trash, but she made sure to leave you here with us, knowing we would love and take care of you.”

"Yes, you do, but the court can take me away anytime, Mama. We must report there a lot and we can't even go out of the city because I am still a ward of the court."

"I am going to do whatever I have to do because you are my child, but she is your mother."

I heard what my mother/grandmother was saying, but at the same time, I didn't. I could not understand why that woman could not love me or most of all want me. After Mama told me that, I looked at her and told her that woman was not my mother—she was, and that if she was to come back, I would make sure she never leaves the way she came again.

Now, understand something—I was six years old, and my mind had already come up with a way to take this woman's life. Once I went into details on how this woman was not going to go out the same way she came in, Mama knew that I needed help, so she took me to a child psychologist, Dr. Bey. I didn't really want to talk to anyone about it; as far as I was concerned, my mother was already in my life. Now since I was only six, I had no choice but to go see this psychologist. She was a nice person but kept asking me all these questions about my birth mother who I didn't know or care to know anything about.

Dr. Bey asked me to draw some things and as I was doing that, she asked me many questions like why I wanted to hurt my birth mother. I told her that she hurt me more than once, so why not? Then Dr. Bey asked me how I came up with the plan to hurt my birth mother. Did someone tell you a story or did you see it on television? I told her no. I didn't see anything like that on television and no one told me anything. It just was the easy way to say goodbye and know I would never see her again. She then asked me why

I wouldn't want to see her. My answer was why would I? Why would I want to see the person who didn't want me or my older sister? How do you come in and out of someone's life and say they're lucky because if you were with me, you would not be alive? How can you love someone who took your family away from you? She doesn't like me or love me, so to me, I think we should give her the same pain she gave us.

I know you want to know how I was planning on hurting my birth mother, but I would just say my mother/grandmother who raised me started teaching me how to cook and told me to always have good manners. I would just have her stay for dinner. . .I think you can let your imagination do the rest.

Now that I am older, I can see that there was something very wrong with me and I had a much deeper hurt than I could even have imagined. I continued to see Dr. Bey. Things started to get strange to me. I started to have all these questions like who my father was. Why didn't anyone want me? As I was getting older, more and more questions started to come with no clear answers. I learned that my mother was an amazing singer who performed in places like The Cotton Club as well as some jazz clubs. I listened to my mother sing because my father had tapes of her. She had a beautiful voice. I did not understand why she would not stay around and sing since so many people wanted to work with her. My mother/grandmother starts having me sing in church. Now I know that also came from my birth mother. I love my mother, father, and stepmother, but most of the time, I was living with my mother/grandmother, my father's mother. Now I need you to keep following me, none of these people are blood to me was my understanding. They were just a family that took my mother in and helped her. They built a relationship with her and that became her family as well, but she just could not stay in one place long.

My mother was not good with reading when she was younger, either so I now know where I got my dyslexia from. To me, that added to the pain in my life. When I was in school, kids would call me a bastard. I did not really understand what a bastard was. When they were calling me one, I would just tell them I was not.

"Is your mother and father married or together?"

"No."

"Do you even know your father?"

"No."

"Then you are a bastard."

That was just another name to show me I was not that important. As I was getting older, my Mama would explain more to me. I started to understand why we were going to court so much. As I learned more, I realized that this thing we call life was not really a friend of mine. I understood finally who my parents were. It was the "ward of the courthouse." I felt that the courts wanted to hurt me as well; they didn't even want me to have my own name. The courts would not even let my appointed guardian adopt me. What type of court system do we have when there is a family that loves you but keeps the child as a ward of the courts?

A ward of the court is someone under the protection of the courts. The ward of the court may have a guardian appointed by the court to take care of the child. The legal guardian is not personally liable for the ward's expenses. A ward of the court will require the court to provide their consent for things as little as going out of the state.

Some people have no idea of the things that the court might have to give consent to. Things like significant medical or psychiatric examination and treatment, marriage, education, residence, or whereabouts, and if you are lucky (which I was not) adoption. Wardship expires when the child reaches the age of 18. When it comes to me, I guess technically the courts were my parents, as I mentioned earlier. Now, the meaning of a foster child in simple terms, is a minor placed in state custody. Foster children are placed with state-licensed adults who care for the child rather than a guardian or parent. Youth may enter the foster system for many reasons; the most common are abuse, neglect, or being in an unsafe home environment. So, the key definition of foster is to promote the growth or development of, to cherish, and to bring up a child. Fostering is the process of raising a child in place of their birth or adopted parents. Foster parents give parental care even though there are no blood or legal ties. Now please understand this is what is *supposed* to happen, but some kids are not that blessed to end up with a family that truly understands the true meaning of fostering a child as Olivia has already shown us. Foster children can grow up in a group home or with a family. Most foster kids end up reunited with their parents, relatives, or guardians. That is why we are so motivated to tell our story, because so many people's voices were taken away. I did not have a choice about being with or without my blood parents. As time went on, there were more things that were revealed. I was playing with my father's birth children and his daughter told me he was my real father. I told her that he was not; he was her father and her brother's father. They were my play sisters and brother. After that, there was a big fight between him and their mother. As the adults were arguing, so were the kids.

"Mama told me I am not their kid, so there is no way for him to be my father."

After a few more words between everyone, their mother burst into the room and told the kids to come on because they were leaving.

***

I never saw them again until we were teenagers. We were in the hospital when my mother stopped a lady with a teenage girl and a baby boy inside the carriage. They spoke for a few minutes about what they both have been up to and then my mother said she has grown up so much and looks so beautiful. After they talked for a few more minutes, they walked off. As my mother/grandmother and I were walking, she said, "That is your father's daughter and ex-wife."

I was like, "Really? Are you going to tell him you saw them?"

She said yes. I would from time to time ask my father questions about that day when they told me he was my father. He looks at me and says, "Baby girl you are my child, but just not by blood. I wish you were, but there is just no way for that to be possible."

I said okay and I dropped it. Time went by and I was around sixteen years of age when I finally asked my father a deeper question. The question came from years of listening to the story over and over, as well as talking to his children who at one point in time had a problem with me. One of them saw me as the reason why their mother and father were not together. I could not understand why the anger was towards me at first. So, once I got home, I went to my father. He was in the room playing his game. I said hello and asked him if he had time to talk. My father stopped the game and told me to take a seat.

"What do you want to talk about," he asked.

"I just kept running over and over what you have told me about my mother, and something just don't add up." I looked him right into his eyes and asked, "Did you sleep with your sister as you call her who was my birth mother at any point in time?" He put his head down with a look of shame.

The next thing that came out of his mouth surprisingly was, "Yes."

"So, you have been lying to me as well as your children this whole time. Your kids are really as they said, my sister and brother."

"No, no, no Baby I did sleep with your birth mother, and I was not with their mother at the time."

I looked towards him and said, "But you could be my father."

"No, the time is off, so there is no way I could be. When your birth mother came back pregnant with you and was telling me you were my child. I did the calculation, and you would have been born already, not still in the oven cooking."

"Why didn't you just go get a DNA test to see?"

"I didn't need one because I already knew she was lying, as well as it did not matter to me either way."

"What do you mean it did not matter?"

"Just as I was saying it did not matter to me because in my mind, you are already my daughter, I don't need a test to tell me that since I am already claiming you."

At this point, I felt as if my whole life was a lie. I really did not know who I could trust or believe when it came to my true identity. I just want my birth rights so I can truly understand me, the person I am, and where I come from. Who is the person I am looking at in the mirror every day? When people go out here and make babies and give them up or abandon them, you really have no idea what truly happens to that child. So, as time went on, more things that were revealed kept taking a piece of me and my life away to the point I wanted to kill myself. So, I will say please think long and hard about what you do with a child you bring into this world. If you don't want that child, make sure you tell him or her the truth because we have a right to know our true identity for so many reasons.

CHAPTER 4

The Dungeon

Tishaee

The new house was more than what it looked like from the outside; the outer view was a porch, two windows, a nice storm door with a screen door and the stucco was and is till this day a dark gray with white trimming. The surface of the inside of the house was just beautiful to anyone who was visiting. However, to me this house became a dungeon for the abuse no one should ever have to endure. I remember one night the parents had gotten so intoxicated that they misplaced house keys and accused my brother and I of stealing them. They kept us up all day and night looking for these keys while beating us at the same time. If it was not an item they misplaced, it was money. I was beaten with a plunger that broke on me which would be the first of many to come.

Do you know what your bones feel like being struck constantly with a thick wooden pole coming down on your body? Let me enlighten you. It feels like your bones are being broken into pieces, but not all at one time. Every hit sends a pain through your joints worse than the last hit. Your body goes limp, you can taste the blood in your mouth as the stick hits your face you can feel the burning sensation of the whelps rising on your body. Then I was put in the tub and beaten with an extension cord. Water and cords do not mix! This type of beating should be outlawed. This type of discipline cuts your skin open with every strike, so badly that it hurts to put any type of clothes on, but I had to. I don't know what hurt more—the beating or the actual clothes on my body. Then it was a rubber hose, or fist and open hand slaps that went on for a week or more until those keys were found. By then, the body damage was done, you can never erase this out of your mind; you can never not feel this pain.

Once the keys were recovered behind and under the back of the television, the lady had the nerve to say, "Oh, I forgot I put it there." No apologizing for the horrific beatings that we had gone through for an entire week or more. This was a repeating cycle. The beatings were so bad at times that one year I missed over 100 days of school. Now this is just a portion of the trauma that I personally endured, but this time, the worst was yet to come and it was an entirely different type of beating. This beating stays with you until you take your last breath of life. If you are not strong-minded, it can and will destroy your world.

The mind can play tricks on you and have you thinking all types of things. For example, "How can I end this beating without hurting me," or "How can I just end the life of the parties causing the beatings?" I had thought about it all, but I was strong enough to think of the consequences that would come with my actions so I just endured what my mind and body would allow me. All this was within the first or second year of them adopting us. Who could we tell? Who was going to believe that these adults were torturing us? The female parent was the one who did a lot of the physical abuse. She was always ready for a fight. She was heavy-handed and when she opened her hand and slapped you, the stars would appear. The slap stung your skin so bad it felt like it was on fire. You did not have time to regroup because another one was coming, back-to-back until she got tired. If I had to say she would be the cause of a lot of the hell that I endured physically. The bruises that were on my body, the broken bones, knots on my head, and the fractured nose—that parent is responsible for it all.

The very first time I saw or even touched a penis I was about seven years of age. I am a kid so you do as you're told but I knew this was not right and should not be done. The first act was getting my adoptive parent off with a hand job and was ordered to never tell. This went on for six months to maybe a year. Every chance he got, and I despised it so much. I tried like hell to avoid him in every way I could think of, but the more I resisted, the more he pursued me. I would cry and plead with him to stop having me touch him in this manner. I did not like it, never liked it, and never will.

My cries fell on deaf ears; he eventually graduated me to the next level, which was even worse. No child should ever have to put their mouth on any human, but here I was officially learning how to give oral pleasure which I despise now in my adult life. I asked him one day why he couldn't get someone in the streets. His exact response was, "They are dirty women and I know you are pure." In his mind it made sense; in my mind, I thought he was sick and crazy. I even threatened to tell the wife (the other parent), along with running away.

He said, "She will never believe you." He was correct on that part, and he said, "If you run away, I will just test out the next sibling."

The one thing I was not doing was letting him touch them, so I stayed and never said anything in order to keep my little people safe. We were all we had and I made a silent promise to them and myself that I would protect them the best I knew how, even if it meant enduring the current beating and any other future ones to come, and I kept that promise to myself the best I knew how.

Whenever he had a free opportunity, I was his for however long he needed or could get. If I was in school, he would pull me out early just for his pleasure. and who was I going to tell? He had already proven his point that no one would believe me, not even the woman who swore to protect and love me under the eyes of God. If you can't keep a promise that you made to the court and God, then all hope was nonexistent for me. In my eyes, God had sent me to hell with no chance to ever survive. When you are young, you don't know much about praying or having a close relationship with God—at least I did not know that at the time, but looking back, I do question why God allowed all this to happen to me. I was a kid. The Bible says in Psalm 37:23 that God has already ordered your steps because He delights in you:

"The steps of a good man are ordered by the Lord: and he delighteth in his way."

Was God not happy with me? Is this the reason why He chose this journey for me? I know every situation works for the glory of the Lord but really, God—did I need this?

Why? Why? Why?

CHAPTER 5

Dyslexic at the Kitchen Table

Lisa

The kitchen table is often perceived as the ultimate place of togetherness to have meals. The spiritual significance of the table is a symbol of family, community, and faithful presence. It's supposed to also be the symbol of our deep desires to be known and most of all loved.

One of my favorite movies that I felt so connected to was *Antwone Fisher*. When I first saw that movie, I really did not know how to tell people what I was dealing with internally, from having problems in school which also gave me even more issues at home. Antwone was beaten and sexually abused so many times he lost count. He finally got away from them and joined the Navy. He deals with people judging him for all types of things due to him being different. Antwone finally gets close to someone that he loves and respects. He feels as though he finally found the perfect family and then in one minute the person he sees as a father says their time has come to an end. He goes off and says no one else was going to take anything else from him or leave him. That is how I felt. People would say they loved me or they will never leave me and I learned that is just not the case.

I also learned that people really don't know what real unconditional love is. The woman I called mother/grandmother loved me but just didn't know how to love me the correct way all the time. My mom did not know how to deal with someone like me. She also had memories of my birth mother that were not all great that she saw in me daily. What do you do when you are told you are like someone that you have never met or even know what the person looks like? I don't even know how my birth mother reacts to things! The teachers had informed my family I needed help with my schoolwork at home. My mother/grandmother would do what the teachers had told her to do. She would tell me to change my clothing and come into the kitchen.

I would sit at the table and pull my books out of my bookbag to do my homework. She would ask, "What do we have to do today?"

I would look at my homework sheet and say, "We have spelling. My first word is 'community.'"

Today I can spell it, but back then I had no idea how to spell or even read it. My mom would get so frustrated with me. If I didn't spell it right when she asked or read and I messed up, she would hit me. I got hit in the head, mouth, and body with all types of things. On a bad and good day, she would read it to me more than once and say, "Now you should have it down," but I didn't. So, I would go to read and miss the second word. I would be dragged from the kitchen table down the long hallway to my bathroom with one hand and the book in the other.

"I am going to give you the book and you're going to read that paragraph again. If you mess up again, I am going to flush you in that toilet until you get it."

I didn't get it, so she kept putting my head in the toilet until she got tired. I think that is one of the reasons why I never learned how to swim to this very day. She didn't understand I would have a real hard time in school reading, comprehending, and spelling.

To give you a picture of what was going on inside of my head, every day was like this: I would go to class. I would go to my seat and look at the chalkboard to see what I had to do for the day. I would pick the easy things I could do so people would not pick on me or laugh at me. I would look at my reading assignments to pick the paragraph that I could get through without making any mistakes when I was asked to read out loud. I didn't always pick the right one to read, so there were still times that I didn't succeed at my goal.

Do you have any idea what it is like to have people pick on you or laugh every time you make a mistake as if they were perfect and I was not? In their eyes and the world, I was also dumb. There was even a time when I thought my mother/grandmother felt the same way about me. I felt this way because no matter what I did, she didn't understand that I had a learning disability. The abuse went on for years.

I still loved her because she loved me enough to keep me, raise me, feed me, and keep a roof over my head. She loved me enough to teach me how to be a woman. She showed me what to do and not to do as a mother. She did all this while beating me with pipes and belts, pulling knives out on me, and forcing my head into a toilet. My mother never saw me speak, play ball, or any of my performances anywhere. If someone thought they could put their hands on me or hurt me, they would be so wrong. She would kill someone over me.

I know what you must be thinking—this woman was crazy. I see why you might feel that way. I really can't tell you what I thought or felt as a child growing up in a house like this, but what I did know I had to be grateful to her for being willing to keep a child that was not hers. I think she did it because she always wanted a daughter and she could not have any more kids. She just did not know she would end up with a kid that had learning problems.

In *Empowered by Disadvantages*, I stated that I was finally placed in the special education program after failing first grade. I tell my readers about this white teacher who grabbed me up by my arm and told me I would never be anything. I wouldn't go to college or even graduate. He told me I would not be anything!

I went on with my education as a special ed kid all the way to middle school. Life for me in school was a love/hate type of relationship because there were people who loved me and hated who I was. I was a popular kid without even trying. So, I guess the kids who did not like me, picked on me because how can a special ed kid get to be on a stage with people like Full Force and opening for them? How does a kid like me get tips from Rob Base; to be friends with DJ Ron G, and Biz Markie (RIP)? I didn't understand how the world of music came so easily to me, but education did not. So, being dyslexic at the kitchen table caused me to dislike the kitchen table—the same table that me and Antwone Fisher looked forward to so we could enjoy those pancakes on Sundays.

19 Or do you not know that your body is the temple of the Holy Spirit who is in you, whom you have from God, and you are not your own? 20 For you were bought at a price; therefore glorify God in your body and in your spirit, which are God's.

1 Corinthians 6:19-20, NKJV

CHAPTER 6

Graduation

Tishaee

Time for another graduation, just shy of my 9th birthday. Sleep has never been meant for me to have. I was jerked out of a deep sleep by my panties being ripped off so he could force himself inside me. The pain that ripped through me is a pain that I can't begin to explain. There are no words on this earth that can help you or me understand, but I am going to try anyway.

It felt as if I was being torn into pieces and the scream that I wanted to let out was like having a baby ten thousand times with no medicine. I tried to scream and fight but I was just too small. He held me down and kept my mouth covered so no sound would come out. The more he entered me the longer the time went on. His body weight was so heavy, and his breath had nothing but alcohol and cigarettes on it and I swear he smelled like piss. All I knew was he was hurting me; I could not fight him off and once again, no one was coming to my rescue. When it was all said and done, he got up and said, "This is our secret."

I just laid there for the rest of the night and when I finally got up there was blood all on the sheets. I got up slowly due to the pain that was going through me. I went into the bathroom and showered, came out, got dressed, and changed my sheets. I tried to wake the woman up to tell her that I was bleeding badly. You know she just gave me the thumbs up and never got up to see if I was OK. Yes, she was in the house when he entered my room and forced his nasty dick inside me. When she woke up, she grilled me about how I now had to be careful of the little boys because my body is now going through a change. I never had the opportunity to even hint at what happened a few hours prior; from that night on I made sure I wore extra clothes to bed. That was the only way I knew how to protect myself. Some nights I was bulletproof safe but most nights the monster won. I could never understand how the woman of the house never heard anything; did the alcohol have her that much in a coma? How do you not see the change in your child? Why do you not see the change? It was so bad that I put little notes around the house hoping she would find one and save me, but instead he ended up finding all of them. When that did not work, I started figuring out how I could slit my wrist, but guess what? That hurts too, and I did not want to die.

She was too stupid to know that it was not my period that I had. However, he came to my rescue to say she is not having sex all the while he was inside of me every chance he got. He said all you have to do is look at her, so they both had me lay on top of the dining table while they took a flashlight and looked up in me to see if I was still a virgin. He was good at convincing her of what he needed her to believe. Somehow, she just never had that woman's intuition, or she didn't care enough. (As I sit here and spill my shameful moments and memories, I feel the tears about to flow.)

At this moment, I now understand the anger that I have in me, but I try not to let it consume me; but deep down it has. How do you bury something so deep that you completely forget what has happened? I have *an* answer, but I really don't have *the* answer. I just know in this moment right here, I am watching my own movie and I want to cry, fall apart, and crawl under a rock. When I come back out, maybe none of this will ever have happened.

How does a grown man force himself into a child? I hear this phrase at times when watching the news, "The First 48," or "Dateline," but I am all too familiar with how this can happen. The real question is what is the thought patterning of the monster? How does a mother not know her child well enough to see the change, the withdrawal, the life that has died within her child? How do you choose your man over your child? How are mothers jealous of their daughters?

Now that she is satisfied, they decide to celebrate, but fun drinking turns into fighting and the police were called. In my mind, I was like, "Yes! I can finally tell," but something told me deep down that maybe I should not. If I don't say something, he will never stop.

So, against my better internal judgment, I told her everything. She hit him on the head with a beer bottle and blood started pouring everywhere. The police finally arrived, and she tells them that her husband has been fucking her thirteen-year-old daughter. We went down to the police station, and I told them everything that had happened. He was arrested, and a restraining order was put in place. I am free, but was I really? You would think so!

Well, it was nice while it lasted. A couple of weeks went by and the house was quiet and safe, but she started drinking again and got upset and started to beat me, saying this is all my fault and that she is not giving up her husband for no thirteen-year-old child.

That is exactly what she meant. She let him come back home and things got worse. The beatings and the sexual assaults got worse, and this time, she was aware of what was going on—she allowed it. She told me when I went to the grand jury to testify to tell them I lied. In the meantime, my insides were being ripped to shreds. Why was this my journey? I may never know.

For I know the thoughts that I think toward you, says the Lord, thoughts of peace and not of evil, to give you a future and a hope.

Jeremiah 29:11, NKJV

CHAPTER 7

My First and Only Male Love

Lisa

Let me tell you about a time when I was dating someone, and I didn't really understand what the new position was supposed to be. I was sixteen years old, and I was dating a basketball player named Richard. He was eighteen and all the girls wanted to be with him. I'm still not sure why I was blessed to get him. It could be because we both played basketball and I really didn't sweat or push up on him. We started out as friends who loved the game of basketball. Our coach would spend a lot of time with just us two. So, we did a lot of conversing with one other that led us to all types of topics. Richard would tell me why he took the game so seriously.

Richard said to me one day, "Lisa, this game is not just a game to me. It's what I was born to do to save my family. It's what going to make me a better man who can spend his time off the court with his wife and kids. I'm going to be that man that comes back to the Police Activities League and helps the next young men make it, like Johnny is doing for us. I know that people are only my friends because they know I am going to be in the NBA."

I told him sure.

Can I tell you something he asked? Richard took my hand, pulled me to him and said, "I like you, and I would like to date you." He then gave me my first kiss in the gym. I was so surprised but horny at the same time. I was not a popular girl that pulled the star players at PAL. Don't get me wrong—I was not ugly or unattractive, but I was a tomboy, so most boys would go for the really girly girl type. In school, I was more popular beginning in middle school and continuing on through high school. But after he kissed me, Richard and I was always together. Richard would come over to talk to my family for hours. That really made me happy. You see, I came from a family who did not play and a grandmother who was super strict was like me winning the lottery, just because my boyfriend was allowed to come over and be in my room. So, to see my family embrace him was so fulfilling. It was a hot sunny day, and we just finished our basketball season, which we both won. I was done for the summer, but he still had to play and practice with Coach to get ready for the tryouts for all the schools that were interested in him as well as the summer leagues. We were so sweaty and tired after the game.

Rich said, "Babe, I'm gonna go home, change, and then I'll be at your house. I really need to talk to your dad about something important and then I have a surprise for you."

I said, "What's the surprise, and what do you have to talk to my dad about?"

He just looked at me with this overwhelming look in his eyes and said, "You'll see. He gave me a kiss on my forehead and said, "I love you. I'll see you soon."

We walked away from each other and as we were walking away, we both looked over our shoulders and waved at each other one final time. I didn't live far from the PAL, so it only took me like 15 minutes to get home. As I walked into my building, all I could do was wonder what Rich had to talk to my dad about. All the talks we've had about him going to college and then pro. I knew he loved me, but I also felt that I could lose him to the pros. As I walked into the house, my grandma was in the living room like always in her colorful house dress. My dad and mom were in the room playing a video game. I gave my grandma a kiss, said hello, and asked, "How was your day?"

She smiled and said it was good, did you win? Now if you remember, my grandmother has never seen me play any sports my entire life. So, before I get off topic. I answered my grandmother, "Yes, we won. By the way, Grandma, Rich is coming over in a few minutes to talk to dad. Is that OK?"

She smiled and said, "Baby, you know that boy can come on over."

I said, "OK, Ma. Thank you. He won't stay too late since he has practice, and I must go to work tomorrow."

My grandma responded with another, "OK, babe."

As I walked to my room to change and take a shower, I stopped by my parent's room to tell my dad and mom that Rich was coming over to speak to him. I was not sure why or what it could be that he wouldn't tell me first.

My father answered with, "OK. What does your man have to talk to me about?"

"I have no idea, Dad."

My father sarcastically said, "You don't know? He didn't tell you it's gonna be a thunderstorm."

"Whatever, Dad. I have no idea, but he'll be over here soon. I'm gonna get in the shower now so I can be dressed when he gets here."

My father laughed at me and said, "OK, Princess."

As I showered, I couldn't stop thinking about what he could possibly have to talk to my dad about anyway. (I am still washing my body as I am thinking about his talk with my father and the kiss, he gave me) I am not sure how long I can hold out from Rich. He never makes me feel like we must go all the way, which makes me love him even more. I know I want him to be the one who I lose my virginity to. I would love us to have a son who looks like the both of us. I don't want him to be like me when it comes to schoolwork and exams; I would love him to be just as smart as his dad is when it comes to the books.

As I am thinking all these amazing thoughts about me and Rich's future and wondering if I am truly ready to give up my virginity to the boy that the whole family likes, I hear the doorbell.

Wow, I am not even dressed! I hopped out the shower, dried off, and got dressed. My father had let him in, and I went into the kitchen to say hi and see what they were talking about. I walked in and Rich stopped talking and stood up to greet me with a hug and a kiss.

I went to sit on his lap, but he said, "Baby, can you give me and your dad a moment? We just started talking, OK?"

"So, I have to go?" I ask. As they both looked at me with their funny-looking faces, I joked, "OK, I see I am not wanted. I'm going in my room."

They both said okay and Rich added, "I'll be there soon." I turned around, shrugged my shoulders, and said okay.

After like a whole hour had passed, it was getting later and later. After two hours went by, I went back to the kitchen where they were just laughing and talking and having a good ol' time.

They saw my face and knew they were in trouble. Rich said, "Baby I am sorry, but it was very important, and it took longer than I expected."

I said, "OK, are you done?"

Rich said, "Yes but Baby my dad called, and I have to get home, and you know grandma and the family are about having me in your room super late."

My dad said bye to Rich with a handshake and a hug and thanked him for coming over. "I truly appreciate you and our conversation. I look forward to when you surprise her."

I looked at my dad with a surprised, frustrated look and said, "You know the surprise too?" So, my father walks out the kitchen. I turned and walked Rich to the door. We stood outside the door talking and as he is holding me, we are kissing and talking.

"So, tell me what is going on."

He said, "I'll make my decision after the two weeks at PAL and the tryouts. Coach says he knows what my next steps will be. Then, we're going out to dinner, and I have a big surprise for you. You know, besides my father, you're the only other person I love and trust. What we have is real, and you're not after my money or fame. Plus, you play basketball. I couldn't ask for a better girlfriend. I love you."

"But there's something we need to talk about. Something I've been thinking about."

I said, "What's on your mind?

Rich laughed. "What do you love about me? Is it my good looks?

I answered, "It's how we always have fun and rarely argue. We both love sports, my family adores you, and you've never pressured me into anything. You respect me, and that's why I want you to be my first."

Rich smiled. "Your father was right. Love must be deeper than just physical attraction. I want the same kind of relationship my parents had. I can't wait for you to meet my dad. He's eager to meet you too."

I said, "And I love that you're willing to wait. When we take that next step, it'll be because we both want it."

I wish I could say everything was perfect after the tryouts, but it wasn't. Rich's father passed away suddenly. I never got to meet him, and it hit us all hard. Rich disappeared after that. He stopped answering calls and didn't show up for practice. The coach and I were worried sick.

Dad said, "Sit down, I need to talk to you. I know you're hurting, but Rich loves you."

I said, "I'm not so sure anymore.

Dad said, "Maybe this will help. Remember when Rich asked to speak with me? He wanted to propose to you after a year of dating. He was planning to include you in his future, give you keys to his place, his car, and even wanted to introduce you to his dad.

I said tearfully, "What did you tell him?"

Dad said, "I gave him my blessing, on the condition that he waits until your 18th birthday.

I said, "Thank you, Dad. That means a lot."

But after my father gave me this overwhelming and amazing news, Rich disappeared. Four weeks passed by. He missed the tryouts, the Coach still can't find him, and I haven't talked to him. At this point, weeks turned into months, and months to years—still no Rich. I realized we were over, and I started living my life, doing the things that I loved to do, and not thinking about any type of relationship. I just decided to focus on working hard on music, sports, and school.

CHAPTER 8

Hatred For Your Child

Tishaee

As a child, you don't understand that your mother hates you. You just figure this is life, but it must get better at some point. Not only did it get worse with the wife no longer pretending about not knowing what was going on—she now partakes in the acts.

Envy is a powerful source of anger. Let me give you the accurate definition of envy: *a desire to have a quality, possession, or other desirable attribute belonging to someone else.* Envision your mother being so jealous of your existence that she is willing to traumatize you in some of the worst ways imaginable to the point where you wish you did not exist; you just want to fall asleep and never wake up again.

The wife hated the fact that her husband was, as she put it, "loving another woman." She beat me every chance she got—every time she knew or thought her husband had his way with me. The whippings were so bad that I ended up with a broken nose and three broken ribs twice with no real medical attention; because she was a nurse, she bandaged me up herself. The thought of her husband touching me sent so much rage through her that she had to watch in order to see what the big deal was. Let's not forget that in the eyes of the law, I was still her child but, in her eyes, I was competition.

I had no emotions—I just had to survive one year, one month, one week, one day, one hour, one minute, one second at a time. During all this time, still no one came to the rescue. Who was I going to tell and who was going to believe me? When it was all said and done, I still had to come back to

HELL, and depending on what I said, would determine the beating that was to come. So, I said nothing. I covered the bruises the best way I knew how: long-sleeved shirts, jeans, hoodies, etc.

The more I concealed, the more she added to my broken body. I ended up with three fractured ribs and a broken nose for the second time which gave me two black eyes from the blows to my face. Remember she was a nurse, so she knew how to cover all this up. I still have the mark on my left leg from where I was beaten with the plunger stick and when it broke on me, she stabbed me with the sharp end of it.

One day, I went to school after being out for over 30 days. My teacher asked me why I had missed so much school. I looked up at her and right as I was about to tell an amazing story, she just happened to touch my arm and I cringed from the touch.

She pulled up my sleeve and asked me how did you get this whelp on your arm? My response was I fell down my stairs, which was partially true. I did fall down my stairs, but I could not tell her I was in the tub bathing and the wife came in with a thick black rubber hose and beat me out of the tub into the hallway, and down the steps I went.

You would think she would have stopped beating me once I met the bottom of the stairs. No, she yelled, "Get up!" and came down and beat me some more until she got tired. By then I had whelps all over my body the size of medium goldfish, if not bigger.

Blood was all over the walls on the steps and on the bathroom floor and all she could say was, "Clean this mess up." (The Real Mommy Dearest).

I did what I was told. My little body had purple marks all over me. To have clothes on my skin only aggravated the pain more. I had to walk around as if I was not in pain. You were not allowed to show weakness because you would get struck more for acting like you wanted someone to have pity on you. That year alone, I believe I missed over one hundred and fifty days of school.

So here in my adult life, I don't show weakness, I show no emotions, I bow down to nothing that I think is a setup. I will hurt you before I allow anyone else to hurt me in that manner ever again or in any way for that matter.

Getting off track for a bit; there was this one time I was not feeling well, and it was time to eat dinner. Now for those who know me know I absolutely hate liver. and I hate Lipton tea; whether it be hot or cold, I hate them both. That night liver was the main course. Now remember I said I was not feeling well, I was told you better eat everything on your plate, the woman knew I did not like liver, but she made me eat it anyway.

Before I knew it, everything was coming back up. My insides landed right back onto the plate. Now a real parent would have given me soup or not made me eat at all. This deranged bitch made me eat the food she said I threw up on purpose. She even made me eat what I threw up. Just typing these words, I want to throw up all over again.

When that did not work as planned, she had me stand in the corner facing the wall for over three hours. I guess it was better than getting hit so I was a trooper and stood strong, but once I was finally allowed to go to bed my little legs were so thankful. If it wasn't her doing the beatings, it was him doing the creeping. I would not call it creeping anymore because she knew exactly what was going on.

It is amazing how you look at a house, a family and you have no idea the horror that is taking place behind closed doors. The saying is so true: never judge a book by its cover.

There were also times when we would not eat for a week, especially the brother and me. This was another form of punishment, but after day two it wasn't so bad. You just stop thinking about food because you would get lunch in school. The no eating part was okay for me again as long as I was not getting beat up, I was cool with not eating every day. However, my brother was not as strong as I was. We found out years later he was sneaking and eating the dog's food. We make jokes about it now, but back then it was surviving the best way you knew how.

Mentally, I did not protect the siblings. As a child, you don't think about that; you focus on what you can see. I did not understand that the mind had to be protected. I failed my little people. I did not do the research on how to protect them across the board. I now know, but it is too late—the damage was done and the cause of the damage was more traumatic for the siblings than I ever knew, but I won't tell their story because it belongs to them, and I will respect that until they say otherwise.

The adults were heavy drinkers. Miller beer and Thunderbird wine were their favorites. It may have started off with just laughs and music, but as the days and nights went on, the atmosphere was destined to change. They turned into monsters. They looked familiar, but they were not at all who they looked like from the naked eye. The music would get louder, the laughs turned into screams, and the calmness turned into a storm. I just never knew which storm was coming.

The nights were always the hardest and the longest; because they were up drinking, I needed to be up with them. Teddy Pendergrass, Whitney

Houston, and Anita Baker were always on repeat constantly. To this very day, I hate Teddy's song, "It Should Have Been You." As soon as I hear this song, I turn it off immediately. I just want to take a hammer to the radio at that moment. I digress…

Back to the facts of this mission. I would be sleep or partially sleep and I hear my name being called over, and over, and over again until I come down the stairs and being told to sit down and watch the drunken dancing, or listen to the music, or the argument at hand for that evening and I better not have moved for anything—not even the bathroom.

The parents were not happy drunks—they were abusive and violent towards each other, so it was only right I guess for them to treat the kids the same way. I remember one moment as if it was yesterday: they had drunk so much that they hid money from themselves—over three thousand dollars. That money was missing for weeks, and my brother and I were beat every day for weeks. Why? Because in the mother's eyes, we had stolen money from her, not that she was too intoxicated to remember she hid her own money. She would hide money from herself all the time. Those few weeks were horrible. I don't even know how we survived—the electric cord, the rubber hose, the plunger stick, the fists, and open-handed slaps were my fate for those moments in time.

Due to the blows my body has taken, I should not be able to tell you this story, but I now see God had other plans for me. For two or three long weeks this money was missing; we looked for this money everywhere, and each day that it was not found there were major beatings to follow or an intense interrogation that followed. The interrogations were so intense that I would just give in and say yes, I did whatever I was being accused of just to stop the torture. I also realized that giving in to stop one thing only led to something else more traumatizing. It did not take me long to stand my ground, take the beating, and whatever the outcome was, so be it.

This is how I also picked up some of my detective skills that I think I am pretty good at as an adult. I learned early in life to never let anyone change my truth, so I have always been known as the child who verbally fought everything. Now as an adult, I am known as the woman who has a switchblade for a tongue. In anger, I say what's on my mind at that moment and I don't really care how it comes across, but you will know what I said is exactly what I meant.

I did not get this switchblade of a tongue overnight. It was developed via hurt, anger, and rage. I will not apologize for that because til this day, no one has apologized to us. Am I looking for one? Absolutely not, but it's the principle behind it. Do I still hold some anger? I would be lying to you if I said, "No I do not." I hold a lot inside of me; at some point, I am sure I will release it all, but in my timing, and not anyone else's. I say this because, in someone else's timing, so much was taken from me: my family, my body, my mind, my spirit, and at some point, my soul. I had no say nor control, but now for the most part, I move to my own set of drums, and eighty-five percent of the time they do not line up with anyone. This is how I now operate; this is what works for me. Everyone deals with life in their own way. My advice to you is just think before you move—a fast move can cost you everything. I will say this again: don't let life control you, because once you do, expect to fail.

CHAPTER 9

The Rape of My Soul

Lisa

It is midnight and I am in my room asking myself how I am going to finally go to a place that I have not been to in so many years. I am crying as I am typing, to find the right words for a person who has been voiceless as long as I have been. I know you must be asking yourself why I named this chapter what I named it. I name it the rape of my soul because it was taken away from me. My mother had instilled in me at a very young age the importance of holding on to your virginity. Now don't get me wrong—I was not a good girl all the time, but I did find a way just like most teenagers to look for loopholes to explore with my boyfriend. A kiss there, touch here; back then we would call it second base, not first.

For those who don't know, first base is holding hands, second base is kissing, and third base is having sex with a person who penetrates your body internally. So, for me to work so hard to stay on the right side of the line not giving my virginity away was very important to me. My first boyfriend was at the age of 13. His name was Jose. My cousin and I were dating brothers and they both were amazing boys. It was the best summer of my life. I had a popular boyfriend who really liked me. All four of us were together the whole summer. I started to get sad because summer was almost over, and I would be going back to my grandmother's for the school year, which meant I would only see him on the weekends. So, in our very last two weeks Jose told me he loved me and that if I loved him, we should go all the way.

Now I know what you are thinking, but it still was something that had me going crazy for the last couple of weeks. I loved him and I wanted to make him happy, but I also thought about everything my grandmother instilled in me. You would think me asking my older cousin for her input she would be like, "Girl, all boys say that," and not to do it. That was not the advice she gave me. She told me I must make up my own mind on this one and if you like him, do it. So, at this point, I am even more confused and unsure what to do than ever before. I even made myself sick over it, but I am happy to say when we met up to talk, I told him that I love you Jose, but I just can't give myself to you in that way, even though I do love you. Jose looked disappointed but leaned over and gave me a kiss and told me it was okay. Once I came back to my grandmother's home, we never talked again. That was the day I learned that boys would do anything to get you to sleep with them. So, when that terrifying day took place, there were so many things going through my head.

You would think that school was fun for the most part, but I have more bad memories than good ones. From middle school to high school there was this boy named Mike, and he would just always pick on me. He would hit me and follow me around the school every minute he could. So, my parents had me transferred to another middle school, which was better. I got away from him when it came to school, but once I got home, I would see him and if he was talking to other girls or his boys, I was okay. He never messed with me when he was talking to the girls, but his homeboys were like a hit or miss. He would call me all types of names and we would go back and forth with each other. It was just crazy—my family would meet with him and finally one day his dad came to a meeting, and he got in Mike's ass about picking on me.

"If this was your sister, how would you like it if someone was doing what you were doing to Lisa?"

After his talk with his father, he didn't pick on me or say anything to me. That was short-lived—after six months his father passed away and two weeks after his father's funeral, he was right back at it again.

I was working late that week and sometimes the elevators were not working. I prayed that this was not one of those nights. What people might not know about the elevators in the projects is that you can stop them from working. Nobody ever knew how they did it, but it was always possible. One day, I got in the elevator, and he was in there with a friend and two other people who were older. The man and woman got off a couple of floors under me. As soon as they got off the elevator it stopped, and the fight was on—if we can even call it a fight since it was one way for the most part. As the inner door closed, he pushed my head right into the elevator wall so hard that I fell to the floor.

"Now what, bitch? I told you I would get you."

I fell right into the elevator door. Next thing I knew, the elevator and I were one for the moment. The next thing that I felt was a kick to my ass, back, and legs that took me all the way down on the floor, face down. If you look at me now, you might not believe that I had long beautiful hair that he grabbed and used to toss me all around that elevator and floor, putting my hands over my mouth. He was so much stronger than me that all I could do was fight to make it harder for him. Once he realized I was not going to make this easy, he used all his strength and weight to be able to pull his zipper down and get to his penis. All I could hope for was that he would kill me after since he was taking away my womanhood.

He yelled at me, "Stop making it worse. You know you want it. But if you don't, I don't give a fuck. If you don't stop, I will have your family killed."

I believed him because he was also a drug hustler who was also friends with the biggest hustlers in the neighborhood. So, I tried one more time to stop him and he slapped the shit out of me.

"I am not playing with you," he said. "I will kill your whole family, so you pick."

He just kept going and going. I just was hoping it would be over soon. How do you take something that is going to change the rest of your life and try to make sense of it? I know you are asking what I mean. I had to pick my family's life over mine.

The next thing I knew was I felt the worst pain I have ever had between my legs. I screamed, but he put his hand over my mouth as he went in and out of my body. I thought, *"Who would enjoy this?"* What I thought would have been amazing when I did decide to have sex for the first time was nothing like I imagined. It was nothing but pain, torture, and most of all the loss of my respect and womanhood. I cried as each moment went by and every stroke went in.

You would think he would be happy with taking my virginity away from me, but he wasn't. He turned me over and fucked me in my ass. I couldn't move. The pain ripped me apart inside out.

As he was releasing himself inside of me, I was like, "Just kill me."

He said, "That would take all the fun out of this. You will never forget me because I will always be your first."

I will not go into all of the details, but there was not one opening on my body that he did not put his penis in. Once he was done, he got up with a smile on his face, and his last few words to me were, "I knew it would be good and if you tell anyone, your family will be dead one way or the other. Try me."

He hit the inside wall of the elevator, and it moved. The door opened, and he said, "Get your ass together. I'll be seeing you again."

I looked at him and I just couldn't move, so he pushed me in my back and off the elevator. The elevators were still not moving. I am not sure who was helping him even on this. Once I was off the elevator, I went to the stairs on the right; he went the other way. I just cried. I can't even tell you how long I sat on the stairs thinking, *"Why I can't just die?"*

It was late, so I knew my family was sleeping. My grandmother was in the living room sleeping and my parents were in their room sleeping. As I watched her sleep for a few minutes, I thought there was no way I could say anything. I walked slowly due to the pain I was feeling, and I was bleeding down my legs. I did the laundry so they would never know. I got something to wear, and I went to the bathroom and took a shower. I just cried. I felt so dirty and no matter how much I washed, I couldn't get him off me, so I turned the water off and got out the shower.

I looked in the mirror and saw no marks on my face, but the pain was still uncomfortable. As I went to sit on my bed and get into it, I jumped right back up. My ass was so sore and on fire, so I got in the bed face down. As I did that, there was flashback after flashback. I went to bed thinking of ways that I could kill him.

Some people say to people who are violated, "Get over it or don't dwell on it." What they don't understand is that it holds on to us even when we don't want it to. You see, as I am telling you my story, I am crying because I still remember the pain that I had suppressed for so long. I was asked to release the secret voice that has been hidden for 35 years. I live with PTSD still to this day. Not only do I have one scar to live with, but there are also two.

The morning finally came, and it is difficult to move or even want to deal with today, but I had no choice. I felt all types of emotions.

I would get up early for school. I am normally a very respectful person, but that day it was very hard. When I got out the bed, I was black and blue on my legs, back, and parts of my arm. I was still bleeding, so my sheets were messed up.

"Damn."

I must change my sheets before going to school. Thank God my mom got me up early. I changed them real fast and got in the shower. I didn't want to do anything but stay in bed and sleep. I couldn't do that because they would know something was wrong with me. I didn't miss school for any reason. I asked myself, *"How am I going to keep a smile on my face? What am I going to do if I see him today?"*

As I was leaving the house, my mom asked, "What is that bruise on your neck?" I said I got it at practice. I was playing volleyball at this time, and my family knew I got hurt from time to time. So that helped me cover up what happened to me.

I had to leave my building every day and did not know if or when I was going to run into him or his mother due to the fact that his mother still lived in the building. I needed to see if I could stay at my friend's house; this way, my family and I could be safe. I knew my friend Debbie would be okay with it and her mother liked me, but the only problem with that is she likes me, and we are in a group together. Debbie never pushes up on me hard because she knew I was not into that, but I had no choice—I must get away from here to keep my family safe and keep me from hurting myself.

When horrific things happen to you the mind can go to a place that it really doesn't want to go but it can come back at any time. I am referring to suicidal thoughts.

I was able to keep the rape from my family for a couple of months, but then he attacked me again. I was coming in from somewhere, was rushing so I did not want to miss the elevator, but there were many people in the hallway who also had to get on the elevator. One of the people was a friend of my father, Mr. David. The others had to get off past my floor, so I knew I would be okay.

I was wrong.

He said, "Do you miss me?"

I turned around and about this time we were in an elevator with people. I hit him as hard as I could, maybe because I felt safe with people in the elevator, but this might be my only time to fight back and maybe survive after all as well as my family because we had witnesses. He went to push me and a person in the elevator stopped him. They started to argue amongst themselves. As the elevator stopped, Mr. David and I went to get off at my floor. Mr. David pushed the door open and I was right behind him. Mike took his size ten Timberlands and kicks me right in my ass again into Mr. David.

The people started yelling at Mike, asking, "Why you kick that girl?"

Mike said, "Fuck you and mind your business if you know what is good for you." Mike tried to get off to hit me again, but this time, Mr. David turned and pushed Mike back into the elevator.

Mr. David says, "I am not scared of you. Hit her one more time and that will be the last thing you do!"

Mike just looks at me and says, "It's not over, but you got this," and the door closes. Mr. David walks me to my door. He was going to tell my father and mother what happened, but I asked him not to. He asked why.

"It's going to get my family killed or hurt."

As my grandmother opened the door, I was crying, and she said, "Baby, what's wrong?"

She called out to my father. He came rushing from the back and Mr. David said, "Dave, that boy Mike was fighting with your daughter as she was getting off the elevator. He kicked her as well as tried to hit on her, but I stopped him. I think you might have to call the police."

I told my family what he did. My family was holding back the tears.

My father was like, "I'm going to kill him." My grandmother said, "Wait son. Let's take her to the police station."

In my neighborhood, it would take forever for the police officers to come. It was easier to just go to the police station. I told my family what Mike told me. My father tells me it would be OK. I looked at my family and said, "Are you sure?"

"Yes, we are not going to let him get away with this no matter what he told you. You know who and what he does. He is not playing around."

My father looked at my mother and Mr. David and said, "I am sure we will be okay. I promise." So, we went to the police station, and they took us back fast to talk to the detectives. I had so many things happen in my head that I could not believe that Mike could finally be going to jail. There was this tall Black man with a suit and raincoat. He says, "Hello Ms. Ward. I am Detective Smith. Can you and your family follow me so we can take your statement?

My father and I walked to the back to the detectives' desk.

"Have a seat. I know this is going to be hard for you and I am very sorry that you have to go through this again but tell me who did it and what exactly happened."

So, I told Detective Smith Mike's full name and what took place word for word, act for act. I had to stop a couple of times due to the flashbacks that I was having as I told him about the day I lost my womanhood. I still remember the look on my father's face as I was telling the detective what he did to me. My father was doing all he could to hold back the tears and the anger.

"I don't know what I would have done if it was my child. no, I do—I would have killed him." The detective said. "Let me see if he has a record and then we will go pick him up."

I looked at him and said, "Are you going now?"

He said yes as soon as I returned from doing a couple more things. I had so many things going through my head. Things like did I just put my family's life in danger like Mike told me would happen or would he finally get what he deserves? I know I was not the only person he did this to. I was asked so many questions from time to time I felt as if I was the person who did the crime when I was the person who had everything taken away.

When the detective returned, he said, "He has a record, and I am surprised that he has not served any time."

I said "That cannot be possible. I know he has."

Detective Smith said, "Well, he will this time because we have you and I will do all I can to make sure this time it sticks."

My father and I thanked him. As we were going to his car, everyone was asking me if I was OK. We returned to where Mike and I lived to see if he was home. I was told to stay in the car as they went to knock on his door. When Detective Smith returned, he stated there was no answer, so let's drive around and see if you see him. We drove around for about 45 minutes—no Mike. So, he drove us back to our home and told us that he would pick him up and as soon as Mike was in their custody and booked, they will call me.

I asked, "Once that is done, what are the next steps?"

"You will meet with the DA and get ready for his arraignment so he can enter a plea. I hope that due to the charges we have on him, they will deny bail."

"What did you charge him with, Detective?"

"There are four counts. First-degree rape, First-degree sodomy, and I don't remember the other two, but I know it was all First-degree charges."

As my family and I were waiting for Mike to be caught, things were off in my family's house. I was not staying there because everyone thought it would be safer until Mike was in police custody. Once we got the phone call saying he was arrested, we all felt a little better in one way. On the other hand, we were looking over our shoulders because we knew he could have anyone do his dirty work for him. Detective Smith kept a patrol car and an officer in the building doing building control. I would go check on my family to make sure they were OK often. I walked in and my grandmother was in the kitchen drinking coffee like always.

"Hey, Baby how are you? Come give me a kiss and hug. I miss you being at home."

"I am OK, mom. I just can't wait for all this to be over."

"How is Mom and Dad holding up? "

"They are OK. He has been in that room for days working on something. I'm not sure what. "

"OK, grandmom. I'll go check on him."

I turned to walk to the back to my father's room and I saw the door was closed, so I knocked. My father says, "Come in."

"Hey, Daddy."

"Hey, Baby girl. How you doing?"

"I am okay for the most part. Getting ready for the studio but outside of that, just waiting for all this to be over with. "

"Have you heard from the DA?

"Yes, just waiting for them to tell me when I have to go to court.

"Well make sure you tell me so I can go with you."

"I sure will."

As I was talking to my father, he was working on a piece of wood. I was not sure what he was doing, but it looked like he was making something. So, I asked what he was working on. I never saw my father working on anything but cars and bikes. So, to see him working on a piece of wood and having all these things around him was shocking.

He says, "I am making an undetectable gun."

If you were there with me, you would see the crazy look that was on my face. I asked my father, "What are you talking about? First of all, why are you making a gun and what makes it undetectable?"

"The gun is for Mike. If I see him in the street, I am going to kill him."

Dad said, "You are not going to see him. He is in jail. I'll just make sure I am ready just in case."

I then asked my father how it works. He had .22-gun shells on his nightstand. Now don't get me wrong; at first, I didn't know what a .22 was. I just saw that they looked like bullets, and I was right. That was the day I learned how dangerous a .22 can be to the human body. My father made a two-shooter gun in his room, and it worked with no problem. I told my father I didn't need him to do anything, not right now anyway because I did not want him to go to jail.

I told my grandmother, and my stepmother knew what he was doing so when he was not looking, she took it and never told him where she put it. She then told him if he was to make another, she would leave. We were just doing all we could do to keep Dad out of jail. Now deep down inside, I wanted Mike to be in jail or killed because what he took from me, I could never get back and I will never be the same. That was the day that made it easy for me to stop suppressing feelings that I was avoiding and feeling that I was not sure why I was having in the first place. The one thing we as women are supposed to love, respect, and marry one day can possibly take your womanhood away. So, why would I ever want to love a man or even spend the rest of my life with a sex that treats women the way they do? That is the feeling he left me with, along with other things.

And we know that all things work together for good to those who love God, to those who are the called according to His purpose.

Romans 8:28, NKJV

CHAPTER 10

Watching

Tishaee

Now that everything was out in the open, the parents were now on one accord. She granted him permission as long as she was informed or able to watch. So, in her mind, it was now not considered cheating. Her exact words were, "Well at least I know he is not out here fucking a stranger."

I currently feel the steam rising in my bones filled with anger. He now did not have to sneak around; he had open access to do what he wanted and how he wanted. This stuff only happens in the movies, but here I was living in this never-ending nightmare. Not only did I have one predator, I had two and they were a couple bonding together. She laid out the blueprints, she watched, she instructed, she got off on it—and I do mean got off on it.

I learned the rules real fast on not saying, "I did not want to do this," or "This hurts so bad." She would just hit me, tell me to shut up, and do what I was told. She said, "You enjoyed my husband in secrecy, now enjoy him in the open. You want to be grown, I am going to show and teach you how to be grown."

Some porn should never be seen live, but here it was, and I was the main attraction. I am almost positive this is not what God meant by, "What's done in the dark will come to light." I truly understood the hate that she had for me and there was no changing her mind that I was not at fault for any of this. All she saw was another woman with her man, not *a* child, not *her* child; but you must remember I was not her biological child. I was a threat to her, and she was determined to destroy me—and she did.

She physically and mentally succeeded. This went on for so long that I became numb; there was no feeling anymore, no more crying, no wishing, no self-love. I was just here for their pleasure and why? Because I had little people to protect, I was determined that he would not touch them sexually anyway. No one should be broken down in this manner: man, woman, boy, or girl.

The husband is a diabetic, so everyone knows the rules of this illness, but do we listen all the time? Of course not! He was also an alcoholic, which is why he started losing body limbs after a while. Alcoholism is one of the deadliest addictions you can have or develop. For one, it is a slow killer. Some side effects of alcohol consumption include the following: Worsening of mental health after the calm feeling fades, hangovers including headaches nausea and vomiting, post-alcohol anxiety, and/or depression. Alcoholism has been known by a variety of terms, including alcohol abuse and alcohol dependence. Today, it's referred to as alcohol use disorder. People with alcohol use disorder will continue to drink even when drinking causes negative consequences, like losing a job or destroying relationships with people they love.

Enough of the mini-education series. He was always in and out of the hospital, which was great for me. Once, he went in there and had bad boils and a yeast ball the size of a grapefruit. Now I did not know what a yeast anything was at the time, but I found out sooner than I needed to. Due to him having this yeast in his system, the wife blamed me for him being this sick.

She said, "Do you know how embarrassing it is to have your co-workers look at you like you gave your husband this germ?" She beat me so badly that I didn't even remember when the beating was over. All I remember is lying on the floor in a pool of my own blood, my head hurting so bad from the bruises I had on my face, and not being able to get up off the floor, but I knew I needed to get up before she came back and give me more of what I had gotten. I have endured more in childhood than most people have in a lifetime. I don't know what strength I had at that time, but I swear I would not be able to handle all this now. (At least I don't think I could.)

As I unveil all that has occurred, I still cannot understand how either one of them thought this was okay, how 1224 turned into a house of horror. I can still see both the outside and inside of the house as if I slept there last night. No one will ever understand what I felt or how I still feel at this moment. I will never know what it means to be pure and innocent because it was snatched away from me at such a young age. As much as I try to understand the thought process of some people, I can't seem to wrap my head around it even with the definition given to me from the suspects themselves. How did God think that these people, this couple, and their thought pattern were OK? I am not saying that I am perfect because I am not, but how do you knowingly harm a child or, better yet, an elderly person? How do you just harm even kill someone, and you just move on about your day? As bad as I wanted to kill them both, my mind stopped me and said, "This is not who you are. Don't do this."

The bad part was I was well within my rights; they would have deserved it, but there was just something that would not let me drop that knife. I saw myself dropping it over and over until I got tired. It would have been easy— they were both drunk and asleep; they would not have felt a thing. Let me take the air from their lungs the way they took my insides and ripped them to shreds. I was tired, sore, hurt, and had no protection; no one protected me; therefore, I must protect myself.

"Shay, you are doing the right thing."

However, there was another side of my mind saying, "No, this is not how this should end."

I don't know if I was just too scared to end the misery or if it was just not in me. I know their time will come; just endure a little while longer, so I listened to the voice inside of me and let them sleep in peace. Later, I would learn why this decision was for the best.

CHAPTER 11

No Justice, No Peace

Lisa

I am at my friend/group member Debbie's house working on one of our songs because we had a studio session the next day at noon. We had to work all night to get ready for our meeting with Atlantic Records. We were so tired, and the limo was coming to pick us up first thing in the morning. As we were getting ready, the phone rang, and her mother called me to the phone. It was the DA telling me that she was no longer assigned to my case, that she got reassigned to another case, and that her boss, the Head DA, was taking my case personally.

"Ok, so will that hold up the arraignment date more?"

She said, "No, everything is in motion and going well. I know you wanted to report to court this week, but now you must wait and meet with my boss who is the Head DA, Kelly Johnson."

I said wonderful and I look forward to meeting with her. "I am sorry you're not on the case anymore. I really felt as if you got me and understood the pain and emotions that happened to me."

She reassured me that the Head DA would also be just as understanding and had many more years of experience under her.

"I want us to make sure he does not get away with what he did to you and if that means I must step down to make sure of that, then I will."

Debbie walked in as I was getting off the phone to ask me something that really surprised me, but at the same time it didn't. Debbie finally took her shot and asked if she could take me out just to put a smile on my face.

I said that I could use a night out but told her that my feelings were all over the place. She told me she understood. Now, I had many emotions due to how I was raised, but I also knew that this was not my first time feeling these feelings. I just suppressed them due to not really understanding why or where they were coming from. Debbie and I were working a lot in the studio and going to school. It was our last year together. A couple weeks passed and I had not heard anything from DA Johnson. Just as I was thinking that the phone rang.

"Hello. May I speak to Ms. Ward?

"Speaking."

"I am DA Kelly calling you about your case. Do you have some time to go over things with me?"

"Yes."

"So, my understanding is that you are a recording artist with a record label. Who are you signed with?"

"I am not signed yet. We are working with Atlantic Records in hopes that we will sign a deal with them.

"Are you still working?"

"Yes, I am."

She then asks me about the night of the attack. After we went over everything, she told me that the arraignment would be in a couple of days. I asked her if she had a date and time so I can make sure I was off work. She told me that I did not have to go. I informed her that the other lawyer, Ms. Walker, told me I would need to be there.

"I have all the information needed and we need you for the trial more than the arraignment and I will keep you posted. I don't want you to have to see him more than you have to. You have been through so much."

I told DA Kelly thank you and I look forward to the update. I also asked her do you think we have enough evidence to get a trial, and most of all a conviction? She told me "I do" but at the same time, she had a lot of questions about my music career which to me seemed a little strange, but I just pushed it off.

DA Kelly asked me one more question before we got off the phone. She asked how likely my deal with the label was. I told her that I was not sure, but I know that they are very interested in my group, and I have a manager and I don't pay for anything. I then asked her what my music had to do with the case.

She then said, "When we go to trial, they are going to ask you about your life and things like that to see if they can make a negative connection about your character and I just want to make sure we have everything covered so my job will be easy. We don't want him to get away with this."

I said, "Fine that makes sense. I had good grades in school when this happened. I have worked since I was 14 years of age and have been in music with some good connections and I have been speaking at events since I was 16 in different cities."

She told me that was great to hear. You would think she was really trying to help me by covering all things. That was so far from the truth. As time went on, I went to see my father and ran right into Mike and his friends. My heart was racing, and I did all I could to not look in his direction too long. He looked at me with a smile and they all were looking at me with a look that I just wanted to get away from.

I rang my mother's doorbell, and my dad answered the door.

"Hey, Baby girl. You, okay?"

"No, I'm not."

I sat in the kitchen and didn't even say hello to my mother/grandmother.

"I saw him, Dad."

"Who?"

"Mike."

"Where?"

"In the back of the building, talking to Tyler and James."

"When you're ready, I'll walk you home. "

I told him okay. I normally say, "I got it Dad," but Mike was the only person on earth next to my mother/grandmother that I was terrified of. There was never a time that I saw him that I did feel normal.

So, after spending time with my family, I was ready to go home. My dad and I left and went out the back door. I asked why we was going this way because we didn't have to.

"I want to see if he is still there."

I knew something was going on with him because he looked way too happy for someone who might be going to jail for a very long time. Mike was no longer there, but Tyler and James were. My father was cool with them, so he asked what Mike was saying. That's when the gates of hell opened for me.

"Lisa, I am sorry, but he is now telling people he did rape you and is saying he is going to get away with it. He is treating what he did to you as if it is a badge of honor," Tyler replied.

My father and I looked at each other with a look of confusion. "Tyler, what do you mean he is going to get away with it? He is celebrating his last court date."

"His last court date? You have not even been to the first one."

"He said you didn't show up and tomorrow is the last day, and the case will be dismissed."

"Do you know what time he has to be at court?"

"I think he needs to be there at 10 am."

My father and I thanked Tyler for the information. Tyler asked my father why Mike was still walking around because if it was my family that nigger would be dead. Lisa, I am sorry that he did that to you.

I just nodded my head. My father and I knew what we had to do next.

"What time do you want to meet?"

"We should get there at nine o'clock so we can see what's going on."

I tried to call DA Kelly. No answer. My father walked me home which seemed like the longest walk ever. Neither one of us said a word as we were walking.

We got to my building, and he asked, "Do you want me to come in with you?"

I told him no.

"You sure you're okay?"

"I am as good as I can be, Dad.

"He is not going to get away with it. That is why we were blessed to find out today so we can stop it."

That sounded good at the time. Once we got there, and found the courtroom he was attending, I asked to speak to the judge, and we told the bailiff what took place and that I was here. Can they tell us what is going on? We were finally able to talk to the judge and see what was going on.

The bailiff told us Judge Black will be with you in a few minutes. The judge walked in and asked me where I had been all this time.

I said, "Excuse me, Judge. What do you mean?"

"You nor your lawyer have been to court."

"I was never told about the court dates and DA Kelly told me I was not needed."

Judge Black had a look of confusion. "I am sorry that you were misinformed, but you were needed from day one. DA Kelly was here and said she did not know why you didn't come. The other days, she nor you were here. Since no one came to defend on behalf of you and the charges he was facing, we had to let him go."

"I want to report her because I didn't know any of this."

He said, "You can try but there is no one in the building that is going to go up against the head DA."

What do you mean? Everyone has a boss to answer to."

"That is correct but before they let the reputation of the DA office look bad, they are going to give you the runaround."

Judge Black did give me the DA office information and told me and my father that he wished us the best, but he had to drop the charges and there was nothing we could do unless he does something else to you.

We walked out of the courtroom to go to see the DA's boss at her office and they wouldn't even let us speak to anyone or even get past security on that floor. We explained why we needed to see her or her boss and they pushed us off and kept saying, "sorry, but no one is going to go up against the head DA." Judge Black did not lie. We walked out of that courtroom with no justice. It was as if I got raped all over again. My father looked as if he wanted to cry for me. That was the day I understood the law, but most of all I learned there was no justice, no peace.

There was no peace within my heart, soul, or body. You see, he left something with me for life, even after all this time. I still suffer from the kick to my buttocks, and the memories are still there even after all this time. I think what hurts the most is he took what he did and was proud to talk about it and nothing was done to him.

The only good thing was that years later the DA was kicked out of office due to interfering and throwing cases. When she was asking me all those questions about my music career, she was doing that because she only took on cases that were high level that would give her the attention she needed to move up in her career. Once she realized that at the time, I was an up-and-coming artist and not the type of case that would do what she needed, she couldn't give the case back to her staff because that would look suspicious. Instead, she just didn't give the case the attention that was needed and she put the blame on me by not telling me that after not showing up all that time, a case could be dropped and that is exactly what took place. I just moved in with Debbie and her mom to get away from him and the building. I am not sure if that was the correct thing to do knowing she liked me, but I just had to get away. My family understood and supported the decision that I had made. I am sure if they knew how Debbie felt, they would have probably found me somewhere else to live.

22 Blessed are you when men hate you,

And when they exclude you,

And revile you, and cast out your name as evil,

For the Son of Man's sake.

23 Rejoice in that day and leap for joy!

For indeed your reward is great in heaven,

For in like manner their fathers did to the prophets.

Luke 6:22-23, NKJV

CHAPTER 12

Court Time

Tishaee

I don't remember the day or time the court hearing was scheduled; I do remember that it was a nice, warm sunny morning or early afternoon. The siblings were off to school. At this time, I was going to the sixth or seventh grade. The instructions were laid out; I remember it as if it was said yesterday.

"Tishaee, you go into this court, and you tell these people you lied. Everything you said was a lie so this case can be dropped. Do you understand me?"

I replied yes and I made sure I followed those instructions. The ride to downtown Camden courthouse was quiet. Finally arriving, the wife and I got out of the car and walked into the building. We checked in, had a seat and from there things were a blur until I got into the courtroom with about twenty-four pairs of eyes on the left side of me, maybe four or more pairs in front of me, and two pairs to my right.

The questions were also a blur, but I do remember saying, "No this did not happen." I said it so much, that the lawyer requested a recess. She asked me what was going on and said, "It's okay for you to tell the truth. I promise you will not be going back there."

A weight was lifted off me. I had only one request before I said anything. "You must get my siblings out of there. That is the only way I am talking."

She promised, and I believed her. For once, someone was going to hear me. I told her the instructions that were given to me. From that moment, I never saw the inside of 1224 ever again.

I was thoroughly examined at the hospital; my insides were so damaged doctors said I may never have kids. I am here to tell you I have three healthy children—two grown young men raising their own families, and a mini-me who I adore, along with three healthy grandchildren.

But let's not get too far ahead of the game. I was removed from the home and placed in an all-girls home. The home was very nice, and the couple were great. I had my challenges there, but overall, it was not bad. There were rules that needed to be followed, for example, you had to go to school every day and you must and will go to church. I believe I was there for maybe two or three years. The girls were cool. I had no issues with the ladies. Of course, we had our moments, but it was a bunch of girls in one house. You expect some chaos every once and a while. We traveled a bit and had summer vacations. It was a normal household: we laughed, cried, screamed, argued, covered for each other—we did normal teen stuff. I attended Hatch Middle School from grades six through eight and graduated in June of 1992. That portion of my life was a success, but I was still missing something. I had to know if my grandmom was still at 2411 of East Camden. It was burning a hole in my soul. I don't know how I got there or what the conversation was to get me there, but before I knew it, I was standing in front of 2411 on a beautiful summer evening.

The fact that I was here was so surreal. What if I am wrong? What if she has moved? Am I sure that I have the correct house? I would feel so stupid and heartbroken if I waited all this time to get to this moment and she is gone. I will never know who or why.

However, I still had not knocked on the door yet. I had this entire conversation with myself while still standing in front of the house. I had made all the excuses I could think of; I said to myself "Shay, just knock on the door. You will never get the answers you want if you don't knock on the damn door."

Finally, my feet were able to move from the spot I was planted in, and my arm went up and knocked. Now whether I knocked once, twice or more I do not know, but I knocked. It seemed like it took an eternity before that front door swung open, and there was this shadow in the dim light yet dark at the same time.

I can remember this moment as if it happened last night. I stood there looking at this woman through my 15-year-old eyes waiting for her to say exactly this: "Yes, can I help you?" (Typing this at this very moment is bringing tears to my eyes tears of joy and other emotions that I can't explain right now).

I said, "Does Mrs. Bernice Arrington live here?"

Her response was, "Who's asking?"

I said, "Her granddaughter Tishaee."

She grabbed me screamed, cried, and stated, "I can't believe you are here!" She held me so tight I did not think she would ever let me go. At this very moment, I now understand how she felt: *"Thank you, God. You did not let me close my eyes without seeing this child first."* I did not know that then, but I now get it.

I met my mother that same evening. I have to say that I was disappointed in what I saw. She was not welcoming and she did not have much to say. She just stood there and looked. I don't know what may have been going through her mind at that time, nor will I ever know.

My grandmom said, "Come hug your child."

I was not there long that evening but learned in that time my grandfather loved us very much and his only wish was to see us before he closed his eyes, but he did not live long enough to see that wish come true.

As time went on, I went to my grandmother's house a lot just to get to know her and learn some things about my past. I remembered some of my cousins, two of my aunts, and one of my uncles. It's amazing what you remember from the age of five years old, but I remember a lot.

However, there was so much I had no idea about nor could I understand the new information. My mom is a legal schizophrenic. I did not know what that meant at the time, and I really did not research the diagnosis either. I know she was not the mom I had pictured in my head. I asked God many days why I could not have a normal family like I had seen so many others have. I don't know if God ever answered my question, but I had more.

My mom was and is very smart, but her brain would and will not compute in the current world; as an adult, I now understand that, but it still bothers me. I suppose that is ok. I would not be human if it did not bother me. Because of the history and knowledge that I now have, I continue to struggle with the fact that she is who she is; some days I am OK with it, and other days she makes it hard for me to deal with her, so I choose not to deal with her unless I absolutely have to. It does not make it right, but like I said she makes it hard to help her. Even with the resources that are out there for her, she is still hard to deal with and the system again does not make it any better. For example, if you need a restraining order, you cannot get one until something life-threatening has happened. I now understand what my grandmom was going through when it came to caring for my mother and I will not care for my mother the way my grandmom did.

Now my sister is amazing with my mom when she has the time to deal with her. My sister has the patience to make her do what she needs to do. My brother and my mom are alike in a lot of ways when it comes to laughter. Mr. C, AKA Bossman (that's what I will call him but those who know me will know exactly whom I speak of). He has a way of making my mom laugh and bringing a little bit of joy to her life. I love the way my siblings have their own way of interacting with her. God did not give me that skill to be able to deal with my mom in that capacity, but what He did give all three of us is a unique strength that was only meant for us.

What I do love about my mom is that you can give her all your appointments no matter how close or how far out they may be and I promise you she does not write them down or anything, but she can remember them to where she tells you a week prior. I don't understand how she does it, but she does it well. So, if you are the type to forget your appointments—tag, she is it. That skill always amazes me. She is far from stupid, this I know, but I must also take into consideration that her brain does not work like the average person, and that is okay. I love her the way she is because I have learned to accept that she is who she is. I would love to have captured her journey to have a better understanding of how and why she is the way she is, but that will never happen in this lifetime.

CHAPTER 13

Connecting the Dots

Lisa

I know people would like to know if I ever saw Rich again. I must connect the dots first before answering your question. The rape happened after Rich disappeared on me. I think that's what made this even harder. I didn't even get to lose my virginity to who I wanted it to be with. I decided no man would ever take anything else from me ever again. When I said this, I had no idea what was to come. I will tell you most victims either don't want to have sex, don't like sex, or become more sexual. I am going to be totally transparent with you. For a short time, I became a more sexual and angrier person. I felt as if this was my only way to be in control since control was taken from me. What I didn't share was that after they released Mike and we were leaving the courthouse, guess who was standing outside?

My father and I could not believe our eyes; it was Rich. He looked surprised and happy at the same time to see me. He gave both of us a hug and asked why we were at the courthouse. I asked what he was doing there and when he got back. Rich told us that he was there about unpaid tickets and he got back a few months ago. Rich looked at me and my father and asked what was wrong. I asked him if he had time to come to my dad's house. He said, "Sure. We can update each other on what has been going on with each other."

Once we got to my father's house, he gave us some time alone. I guess he knew I wanted to be the one to tell Rich about the rape. It took me and

Rich a couple of minutes before we started talking to each other. We just looked at each other for a few with a look of love. Where do we even start?

So, Rich took a deep breath and said, "I know I owe you an apology for just leaving. I just had to go. Me losing my father so suddenly was just so overwhelming and I didn't know how to love or trust anything. I am so sorry I hurt you. That was never my intention. I saw us getting married and having a family."

I said, "How could you just leave me like that? We were a team. I would have never left your side."

"I know, but if I had stayed, I would have hurt you unintentionally."

"I guess I understand. So how have you been?" He told me he was doing good for the most part. "So, you look good."

I told him thank you. So, why was you at the courthouse? I was there to stop the person who raped me from walking on the charges. The look on Rich's face when I said rape was a look of hatred, anger, and pain all in one. I knew he really loved me when I saw the tears in his eyes. The next thing I knew, he jumped up and yelled, "I'll kill him!"

I was surprised and not surprised at the same time. He asked me to tell him what took place. All I could do was cry. I told him what took place and he just held me in his arms. I still felt safe in his arms—probably safer than I have ever felt in a long time. I still didn't tell him about who I was talking to at the time; I thought that would come later. Rich and I started spending time together all over again. It was just like old times.

I wish I could tell you it lasted, but it did not. Rich did just like he did the last time. He just disappeared again with no communication at all. I was hurt, but not broken this time.

I will never love another man like I loved Rich, but I also forgot about the other side of me that when I was with him; it never really came to mind. Rich helped me not think about it or maybe I was just feeling voiceless because I had to. You see, after the rape, I tried to go back to a somewhat normal life: I was in the studio, going to school, and trying to put Mike and the rape behind me. I didn't even like going to see my family because I really didn't want to see Mike.

I started talking to someone and I thought I was happy, but what I realized was that I was ignoring the red flags because I couldn't go back home. So, what I thought was love and happiness was just another way of being trapped and abused. Now, if you remember my mother/grandmother was physically and mentally abusive to me intentionally and unintentionally. I mention this because of my mother/grandmother's abuse and the rape I didn't see things clearly. So, again my voice and mind were trapped.

I could not end this chapter without admitting that I did see Rich one more time—can you believe it?

It was summertime and I had gotten into the habit of going to the movies by myself. That is a habit that I have learned to enjoy very much. All creative people have something that stimulates them. One of mine is going to the movies alone. It's one of the places that arouses my creative flow. I either get my creative ideas in a dream or when I am at the movies most of the time. I feel God has my full attention of my mind.

So, let's continue, as I was looking to find a seat, who do I see on his phone alone, talking? Now, you would think the theater had a lot of people since I stated I was looking for a seat. It was like five people in the theater, but you know you must find that perfect spot to watch the movie. Like always, we were surprised to see each other. He got up, gave me a hug, and said, "What are you doing here?" I said, "I can ask you the same."

We just started talking and laughing. Now mind you, he is still on the phone with some girl. He kept telling her to hold on. I started to hear her yelling at him, which I could totally understand. He asks me to give him a minute. He is telling the person on the phone to calm down you have no idea who I am talking to, and I have not seen her in years. She is very important so if you do not give me a minute, I am going to kiss her and hang up this phone. I was looking at him as if he had just lost his mind to be telling her this. She continued to yell and scream at him over the phone, and he did exactly what he said he was going to do. He put the phone to the side, turned to me, and gave me a very deep and passionate kiss. He then said goodbye to the person on the phone and dropped the call.

I asked him if it was his girlfriend on the phone. He said no it was just someone he was talking to, but they were not exclusive. I told Rich he was crazy and that was not nice.

He stated, "I told her to stop."

We watched the movie together and we spent the rest of the day together. His phone was continuously going off, but he never even looked at it.

I said, "You sure you don't want answer it?" He said no.

After the movie was over, he came over to my place and we talked for hours. He still looked amazing, and he was able to bring out the feminine side of me instantly, tomboy girl and all. As we were walking to my place, we held hands. It was just like old times.

One thing I can say about Rich, he was always protective of me. We were walking to my place and we both knew a lot of the same people. People were shocked to see me holding Rich's hand. We said hello to some, had small conversations with others, but in that moment, I knew he still cared very much for me. He told the people we did talk to if he was not with me, and they saw anyone messing with me for them to step in. He told them I was his girl no matter who you see her with, protect her for me. They told him you got it.

We finally made it to my place. He said, "You are doing good for yourself. Nice apartment."

I said, "Thank you. Have a seat and make yourself comfortable. Would you like something to drink or eat?"

He said, "No I am good. Come sit down with me. Let's continue talking. I miss you."

As we were catching up, I learned he had two children, a boy and girl. They looked so beautiful. I would be lying to you if I didn't say I felt a little disappointed as well as jealous.

I asked him was he with the mother.

His response was, "No. We did not get along, but we are very good with co-parenting."

I said, "That's good. I am so happy for you. I knew you would make a great dad."

He said thank you.

"So, what is new with you since the last time we saw each other?" I thought to myself, how will he handle the news that I am bisexual and I am dating a woman? Now in my mind that is what I thought I was since I was attracted to men and women. Surprisingly, Rich took it extremely well. You see, Rich in some form blamed himself for me being attracted to women since he was not here to protect me from the rape. I think Rich felt as if I was never raped, I wouldn't even be looking at women at all.

We talked some more, and it was getting late. He asked what I was doing the next day. "I am going to a club. Would you like to go? an all-girls club." He said sure what time do you want to meet up.

I said are you sure. Rich looked at me and said I love you and I will always support who you are. We hugged and said goodnight. We talked for the whole summer. He even met the woman I was talking to at the time. They got along and they were both respectful to each other. You see, she knew who Rich was, so there was no need for any additional conversation. We had a good time at the club. He just sat at the bar and watched me enjoy myself.

Me and Rich never had sex. After spending the whole summer together, Rich and I had our first disagreement. I was going somewhere, and I ran into him and another woman. That didn't bother me—it was how he was acting that did. I don't remember everything. I know we walked away from each other unhappy. I never saw Rich again.

Even though Rich and I's last meeting was not a great one, he is still the man I will always love and respect because there is no doubt that we loved one another. Life just took us in different directions, and I know that I wouldn't been able to be the woman that he deserves and I think Rich also felt the same way. All we could do was love each other for the moments and time we had.

CHAPTER 14

Reunited With the Real

Tishaee

Before the summer was over, I moved in with my grandmom, mom, and two cousins. My caseworker at this time was Ms. Rachel Murray. She was amazing, and my grandmom loved that she was on top of her job. It was suggested that I go to therapy, but I was so against that. why should I need to do therapy? I lived the horror. Now don't get me wrong; I am not saying therapy does not work, it was and still is not for me.

My grandmother had rules that I needed to follow, and the main rule was I better not come up pregnant because if I did, I would be kicked out of her house. She was very old school and meant what she said. I adjusted well there for the most part, but I had a hard time understanding why my mother did not keep us and what was wrong with her at the time. The one thing my mom was able to tell me was that I had been spelling my name wrong for years. I had always and was taught to spell it "Tishee." Come to find out, the correct spelling is "Tishaee" My middle name was given to me by my godmother who I have never met which was and is "Olivia.".

I learned that my mom was not well and had not been for years, but in my young mind, sick or not, all mothers wanted their children. I could not get past this; as a matter of fact, I was angry with my mom for years. Even now, I am still angry with her, it can almost be to the point where hatred sets in. I would ask her certain questions and she could not answer me, or in my mind, she would not answer me. This angered me. I was told that my family loved us, but that was not good enough for me. In my world, the family did not fight hard enough. In my teens and young adult years, I despised my family because I felt they just threw us away. My family has no idea what we went through. They may find out now, but the damage is already done. But I have a couple of wise friends that are very close to me who said, "Liv, you must forgive not for the individuals, but for yourself." They were correct, but it has taken me a bit to completely get to this level when it comes to this part of my life.

I went to Camden High School and did what was required. I worked a part time job at Burger King, ran track for a year or two, did physical fitness, and was part of the marching band. I did all this up until my junior year when I met my son's father.

I was not a perfect teenager, but I did my best. My grandmom hated that we were a thing and she tried everything she could to make sure we were not an item. Before I knew it, the two of us became three. Anytime I was testing for any subject I would get sick, or my stomach would hurt. this time my stomach was hurting and yes, I had a test coming up, but this was different. So off to the hospital we go. We get there, and tests are run.

I was in this room alone. Finally, a doctor comes in and says, "You are pregnant, young lady." I looked at her and said, "I can't tell my grandmom this." I asked the doctor to tell her for me.

Now remember her rule was if I popped up pregnant, I was out, and she meant that. She was so upset with me. She said she wanted to push me down the basement steps, and she attempted to bring what she said to life. She told me that I would not graduate and that I was not staying with her. I ended up at my aunt's house during the remainder of my pregnancy. I was unable to stay in school because I was pregnant, so I was homeschooled until a few months after the baby was born.

I had my first child on January 20, 1996, at 11:50 pm via c-section in the middle of a blizzard, the worst storm we have had in years. This beautiful baby boy forever changed my life. At that moment I knew that this child would never go through what I went through, and I would give him the best love and care that I could give.

Six months later, I graduated with that child on my hip. I had proved my grandmom wrong because I finished high school. She was not there to witness it because she chose not to be there, but I succeeded in what she said I would fail at, thanks to the help of my aunt, and my son's father's side of the family.

Two years later, I was a working mom with two bouncing baby boys. At the age of nineteen, I had my second child on December 20, 1997. As a mom, my journey was not easy. I will be the first one to say please wait if you can help it to start a family. Single-parent life is not for the weak. Babies need a lot of attention, time, money, and resources that can be hard to come by if you do not have the best support system. I remember catching the bus, the 405, 406, and 407; my Jersey folks know what it was like. The 405 went to the Cherry Hill Mall. The 406 went down Marlton Pike, and the 407 went to the Moorestown Mall. The memories! I had to take the baby out of the stroller, fold the stroller, load it on the bus, and guide a toddler, but I made the best of it and kept it pushing. You have those days and nights where the baby is sick, and you must call off work, doctor visits, the cost of childcare which was thirty-five dollars per week, and Pampers were twenty dollars a case during my time, which seemed like a lot but looking at today's price I had it made. I worked, managed a household, and still figured out life.

My original goal was to go into the United States Air Force and make a career out of it, but my little bundle of joy came, and I did not have the support system I needed to live out that dream. Do I have regrets? Yes, but I also was responsible for the choices that I had made and that was to become a mother. Let me make it clear—I do not regret having my kids, but I wish I had just did life a little differently versus life doing me. But you live and you learn; take one day at a time and one motion at a time. What you think may be a wrong turn in life trust me when I tell you God has a way of always getting the glory out of it just hang in there. Don't throw in the towel; you must travel this road. God equipped you with the skills to complete the assignment(s) you are facing—all you have to do is trust the process. No, it will not be easy, but life is not going to be at times. If it was how are you going to know how strong you really are? Take what I say and evolve. You've got this! I believe in you. Most of all you are uniquely, fearfully, and wonderfully made because that is how my God made you and He is never wrong. If you don't believe me, try reading Psalms 139:14:

I will praise You, for I am fearfully and wonderfully made;

Marvelous are Your works,

And that my soul knows very well. (NKJV)

CHAPTER 15

The Kidnapping

Lisa

In the chapter called "My First and Only Male Love," I stated I tried to go back to a normal life, and it was somewhat normal, but I had no idea what was to come in my future. I was at Debbie's house, and I told her I would be back after I was done at my parents' house. I also had a meeting uptown. So, I went uptown first to take care of some business.

Now, I must say I really don't recall much of that night. I will tell you I woke up in a dirty alley under a building with my pants down, shirt open, and water around me on the ground. It was also daylight. I was hurt and couldn't move too well. I made it from the alley to the street. I don't remember how I got to the police station or hospital. I was told that I was missing for not quite 24 hours. I remember being examined at the hospital and I think pictures were taken. The biggest thing I remember about that night was my family seeing me in the hospital ER and the nurse giving me a commonly used treatment called levonorgestrel. I asked what it was for. She told me that it was used to prevent pregnancy if it is used within 72 hours of sex. I had no problems taking it since I did not want to get pregnant in that way. Debbie and I got into a real big fight at her mother's home and were told we had to leave and go back to the projects. You heard me right, back to the same place I was raped. So, my family took us both in because they didn't want to see Debbie in the street. I didn't see Mike, which was great—thank God! We had been there for some months now, saving money to move. I was not doing that great after the kidnapping. I was moody for a lot of days. My mother/grandmother was asking me what I would do if I ended up being pregnant. She asked me this because we were waiting for the pregnancy test to come back. They had informed me that the medication might not work, and there was still a slight possibility of me ending up pregnant. She was asking me what I was going to do because my mother/grandmother wanted me to keep it. I was like no way in hell would I do that.

Why would anyone want to keep their rapists' baby? I know there are people who would. I commend them because it takes a strong woman to be able to do that. I just did not feel as if I was one of them. So, I would pray I was not pregnant. We were still waiting for the test to come back and one night I woke up, went to the bathroom, and realized I was bleeding heavily. It was not my menstrual time. My mom said that it was the levonorgestrel working. Weeks later, I got a letter under my parent's door from the hospital, but the envelope was ripped open, and it was empty. We also saw that Mike had returned. Then me and the family started putting the pieces together. We had no way of proving that he had anything to do with the kidnapping but in our heart, we knew it was him. He had hurt so many other girls and this was his style. I was so scared of Mike, not knowing if he would hurt me again. I just needed to get away as soon as possible. I felt so trapped I thought about taking my own life. I had my friend's gun. He had asked me to hold it, so he could show me more about holding the gun when shooting. So, I went to the roof and just stood there holding it, thinking about pulling the trigger and ending it all. If I did that, there would be no more pain. I couldn't do it, so I just cried. I learned that I had PTSD and needed a lot of therapy. What do you tell someone who has been raped, physically and mentally abused, abandoned, and kidnapped? How can you tell someone to get over something like that? I would tell you to think about if it was your child or family member would you feel the same way? We need to speak up if we are going to make a difference in helping other young people not have to go through what Olivia and I did.

CHAPTER 16

Street Life (Off Track A Bit)

Lisa

My street life was very short. People join the street life for so many reasons, but the reason I got into the street game is because I wanted to take care of my grandmother and father. I also wanted to have a life of not worrying about where my next meal was going to come from. My grandmother did all she could to keep me from the street life. I never really played outside unless I was at my father's house. I had a good friend who was in the game who I could go to and as I think about it, I knew many people in the street life because they were my protectors since I was the good girl who went to school, worked, and really didn't talk to the boys in the projects too much.

I was able to talk to the drug dealers about anything. I learned that they were very intelligent people which made it even harder for me at the time to understand why they were in the street life. They all had the same answer for the most part and that was to take care of their family like a grandmother or mother. Back then, most fathers were not in the picture and the sons had to step up to be the man of the house. So, I guess our reasons were not so different after all. I went to my homegirl Shelly who had been in the streets for many years. She was a little thing, but she didn't take any shit from anyone. She was also gay, so I saw a lot hanging with her. But let me stay on topic. There was a guy named Tim who I had known for many years liked me. I was not into him like that, but I could always go to him if I needed anything. I thought he was my friend. So, I told Shelly about Tim and since Shelly's supplier was no longer in the game, I told her I had someone who could give us what we needed and I have the workers as well. Would she be willing to do this with me since I am new to the game? Shelly with no hesitation told me she had me. I had no worries about Shelly—we always looked out for each other and when anything went down, we had each other's back. Shelly and Tim asked me individually, "Lisa are you sure about this? This is not you or your lifestyle."

"I am sure. My grandmother needs the help. She is getting older and the money from work and music has not really kicked in like it should and my dad is doing his own thing. He helps when he can and now that I am older, I have to step up and take care of this woman who did not have to keep me or look out for me at all. I love her and it's the right thing to do. So, you got me."

Shelly and I got about $300 of work and flipping it would give us $3000.00. That was just for my workers, but Tim had our big weight of about $5000.00. Tim was going to go to Philly because the money was better there, and it moved faster. I wasn't a dealer that sold to the people in my community, and you had to be an adult; I didn't sell to kids at all. So, we went to the non-Black communities or areas that the Black people did not go to buy. Kelly and I both agreed with that. We would meet up with the crew, give them their supplies and instructions, and we would hit the strip. Things were going okay for a couple of weeks, but on this one day, when they had to do a drop to me and Shelly, they got spotted and we had to run and separate, and the worker had to get rid of the work. Me, Shelly, and two more workers got away, but one of our boys was arrested. We were not sure if he was going to talk or not. We also didn't know how much work he had on him. I was personally worried because I would have to tell his grandmother. After a week or two had passed, we got a call, and our boy was released with no charges at all. Shelly was like he still must give us our money because he got arrested for not listening to our instructions. He understood and told us he would repay our money by working it off. We had to tell him that was not possible and that he was no longer good to us.

I will tell you that we never got our money from him nor the other kid but that is not what really stopped me and Shelly from the street life; it was Tim.

We called him and told him what happened. He was like, "Don't worry, I got you and you will not even miss that $3k that young blood lost."

I was like, "Thanks Tim. Shelly and I really need this money, and this has to work."

When will you be back in town," he questioned.

"I'll be done and ready to go again on Friday but if you want to double up then give me two weeks and if you give me three weeks, I will have your $20K."

I talked to Shelly she said that would be the smart thing to do so we told him we would see him in three weeks. Shelly and I were not worried because we knew his whole family. He was our friend.

I learned after a few weeks that you really don't know who to trust. I already had a problem with trusting people due to the fact that if your own mother does not love you enough to keep you then who can you really trust 100%?

The next thing I learned changed everything in my life which was the next major move that Shelly and I had to do. I am grateful for the spiritual seeds that my mother/grandmother gave me. You see, the major thing that changed was that Tim called us and said everything went well and we would see him on Friday. Friday came and went, and there was no Tim. Two weeks passed. Me and Shelly went to his mother's house to see his brother to get an update. He told us he had talked to him every day and was on his way home the next day.

I told his brother, "I really don't want your mom to have to lose her firstborn, but if he is not back with our money tomorrow, whenever he gets back, he is ours."

His brother responded, "Lisa; I understand we peoples, but are you really ready to do this?"

I stood eye-to-eye with his brother, Shelly at my side and said, "I am not the one to fuck with. I am a good person, but if he thought he can rip me off, he must not really know I am that bitch no one wants to cross. We peoples, but your brother forgot that, so I'll see you at his funeral to pay my respects and pray that you don't try to make a wrong even more erroneous. Don't think just because we are women, we won't go there because you would be highly incorrect."

I started to walk out of the room and Shelly was right behind me. We looked back and showed him the guns that we had on us. We then said good night to his mother and left. I didn't sleep that whole night. I just kept saying to myself, "Can I come back from this?"

My father knew something was wrong. He kept asking what was going on. I decided to tell him because I didn't know if I would see him or my grandmother again.

He said, "Baby what are you going to do?"

I said, "Dad, let's just pray he comes home tomorrow and have our money because if he doesn't, then you might have to come to the jailhouse or my gravesite."

My father talked to me for hours to try and change my mind, he told me that we would be okay and that I didn't have to do this. I told him it's already done I don't mess over people, and I am not going to let anyone take from me or my family. I got up from my father's bed and told him I can't make any promises. all I can say is that we will see what happens. I didn't sleep a wink that night. I was just looking up at the ceiling wondering what was going to happen tomorrow. Shelly called to make sure we were meeting up so we both were packing. The next thing I knew the alarm went off, and it was time to get ready for work and meet Shelly afterwards. The entire day, I was walking around in clouds wondering if I would be back in this same place tomorrow or would my life be a life sentence from a jail cell. Time was moving in slow motion all day but 5 o'clock finally came and I was on my way to meet with Shelly. As I was waiting for the train, I called Tim's number one more time, praying he would answer the phone. My call went right to voicemail. I then called his brother to see if he spoke with Tim. The phone was ringing, and he picked up.

"Hey."

"It's me, Lisa. You talk to your brother?"

"Yes, he will be home today."

"Does he have my money?"

"I don't think so, but Lisa please don't hurt my brother."

I just hung up the phone. All I remember thinking is, "This is really going to happen. I am going to have to take a man's life! God, can I even do this?

I rang Shelly's doorbell.

She answered, "Come in." We walked past some of her family members who were in the living room. We finally made it to her room and closed the door so we would not be interrupted as we loaded up our guns and our extra bullets. We wanted to make sure we had enough if things really went down. We got a cab, took it to Tim's house, and sat in front of his building. As we were sitting there, crazy me was asking God to send me a sign so I wouldn't have to kill this man. The next thing I knew, a cab was pulling up to the building. Shelly and I looked at each other and put our hands on our waists where we had our guns.

I guess God heard my prayers; it was my father who stepped out of that cab. My father said, "If you are not going to leave, then I am not going to either." We sat there until midnight, but Tim never came home. Shelly and I looked at each other and decided to go. My father didn't say anything; he just walked with us as we walked away from Tim's house. Weeks later, we went back to his home, and he was there he let us in. We went to the back of his house. We asked Tim where our money was. He gave us a bullshit story about getting mugged. We told him he was a lucky man if he had come home that night, we were going to kill him. Looking into our eyes, Tim knew we weren't playing. He just started to tell us he was going to get our money back. I realized a couple of days later that this is not the life for me and that I will always be grateful for what we had at one point, but from this day forth, we will never speak again. I was ready to take your life and do whatever time was given if I was to get arrested. This street life is not for me. I am not the person who wants to kill someone because they feel like they want to keep testing me or take what is mine. I know me—I would if I must, but that is not the life or the journey that I want to be on.

That was the day I knew that the street life was no longer for me. I know you must be saying I can't even imagine Lisa in the street game, you wouldn't be the only one. What you might not know is that when you get in the street game, most of the time you work for someone. I came out of the gate working for me. I was a boss even in a life I never really wanted to be in. I mention this because you are who you are. If you are a leader, then you will lead in everything you do. You just need to find your calling and journey.

CHAPTER 17

The Dirty Thirties

Tishaee

At the age of 30, I had my final child; my only precious baby girl who stomped into the world on her brother's 11th birthday December 20, 2008. I never wanted a girl for reasons you are now aware of. On August 20, 2008, her father and I found out she was a girl. I cried for a long time—so long he said, "Get it together before my child comes out depressed."

Not that boys cannot be harmed in the same manner, but me being a female I knew the history, and I was determined that not having a girl would be less stress on me. But as you see God had other plans and I am glad he did!

I can say that my baby girl has made it to the age of fifteen untouched. But let me make it clear—if she had been or is ever violated in any way, I promise you the individual will be carried by six! They will never see the inside of a jail or a courtroom and this is not a threat; I mean this with all my soul.

I have always kept an open line of communication with my children. They understand that no matter what it is, they can come to me. Will I yell and ask questions? Of course, but they should never be afraid to speak with me about anything. I leave that door forever open; it is up to them to use the resources that are before them. With that being said, I am proud of myself as a parent. I was not perfect but what parent is? I have never had to visit a child in jail, see a child on drugs, or not being a productive citizen. As a parent, I am truly thankful for that; I did what my parents could never do, and that was to be a parent.

I have been married more than once. I have learned what I want and do not want in a marriage. I will say in the next life, I will stay single. Marriage can be a beautiful thing if you are with the right person. You both must put God first— if you don't, then the relationship does not work, I have learned this the hard way. You both need to have trust and be secure with one another and lastly, you must be willing to put in the work to have a successful relationship. I won't go too much into that part of my life because some things you should keep for yourself respectfully.

I am self-taught in Sign Language and still learning. Sign Language has always been a beautiful, yet unique language. I was first introduced to this beauty in church. at the Resurrection Center and still attend this amazing church till this very day. I joined the sign language ministry that was formed and so glad that I did. I learned so much in this ministry. The culture of the deaf community is indescribable; it's a hidden language that is slowly coming into its own. Sign Language allows me to commune with God in a way that gives me a calming sense of relief.

When it's time to minister, I just ask God to take over as he sees fit. This is how I met my Godbrother Thyson; the gifts God has placed inside him he shares with me. He is my mentor when I need to vent spiritually and personally. I can say at any given time, "Hey I need to bend your ear." His response is always, "Liv, who do you need? Your brother or the pastor?" I could write a book on him and our relationship, but that would not come close to what he means to me.

I am also a model for the infamous "Frame of Elegance" photographer

Michael Robins. We have been on this journey of photography and modeling since 2013. We have learned and progressed together. I can look back and see the confidence and the growth of who I have become as a woman. Most people hate taking pictures and I used to be that person, but I am not any longer. I believe in creating memories. Life is short, but memories are forever.

I am the ambassador for Douglas Exquisite Fashions by Carolyn Douglas. This lady has been dressing me for years and I have never been disappointed in my look! She does me right every time and all the time. I am also an ambassador for the brand-new clothing line Avodgy & DoKRoC for Lisa Ward and Jamil Bey. There is more to come working with them for sure!

Finally, I am an author. I want to be the first to say that I did not want to write this book for many reasons; my life did not need to be put on display. I will say I felt pressured a bit, so I thought long and hard and still don't really like the idea of my life being on display but who else can recap my life better than me?

I battled with myself back and forth to get my emotions and fears on this paper. Finally, I caved and said, "Tell your story. You never know who you can encourage, who may heal from your trauma, and who may need to know that ending it all is not the answer. You were built for this, and you will survive! Life is and always will be a teaching moment. You must decide to learn from these moments or let them consume you. Never give up; you don't know how strong you are until you have gone through and completed the battle. There will always be the war of life, but you fight one battle at a time."

I always say to step back, take a moment, breathe in, and exhale. Try to never react in anger. Yes, this is sometimes easier said than done but take one day at a time. You should never let anyone or any situation take you out of your character, because once you do, they have won. You must be willing to conquer this thing called life every minute of the day. Why? because you are God's child, therefore you are more than you give yourself credit for.

CHAPTER 18

Music, Money, and Manipulation

Lisa

When you listen to people like Marvin Gaye, Usher, Kirk Franklin, and Tamela Mann, their music speaks to you in so many ways. Some of these artist's music have saved lives and some have been the voice singing when a child was conceived. Music is a powerful instrument. Most people have no idea just how powerful music truly is. If you look at it from a medical perspective, according to research from Northshore University Health System of Chicago, "Music stimulates memories that wrap themselves around us; it increases levels of serotonin and endorphins, which in turn elevate moods and relieves depression, anxiety, and pain."[1] Music also reduces blood pressure, improves sleep quality, mental alertness, and memory, and lowers the stress chemical cortisol.

The power of music is so impactful to the world that Lucifer/Satan was a music leader in charge of music in Heaven. In addition to singing, Revelations 5:8 and 15:2 mention harps used in the worship of God. Worship of God in Heaven will include singing as well. Even Satan served as an angel before the Lord. If one of God's angels used music to turn people to His side, it shows us that without God, we can fall for anything and anyone. I touch on this and show the other side because music is something

---

[1] "9 Health Benefits of Music. Northshore. December 31, 2020. https://www.northshore.org/healthy-you/9-health-benefits-of-music/.

I choose to use to help communicate my feelings, thoughts, and emotions. I use music to teach love. Once I got older, my family told me that my birth mother was a good singer. I then started to understand why music was my go-to whenever I was in pain. Music was like life and air to me. It came to be something so natural for me to do. I didn't understand how understanding music was as easy as speaking English to me. I knew by the age of 14 or 15 I wanted to be an entertainer on stage, making people feel good when they were hurting. I had a big audition to sing for a man named Bobby who did a lot in music. If he liked you, then he would help you meet the right people. I am not sure how Mr. Bobby heard about me, but he was open to hearing a demo of my work.

I was always a child who had issues with her tonsils all the time. This time, it just came at the wrong time. I had just one or two weeks to get my demo to him and my voice just was not cooperating with me. If anyone reading this book really knows me, I was not going to miss this opportunity. I saw the doctor and was told not to do any singing for a couple of weeks or until the swelling of my tonsils went away. I did not listen to my doctors or my parents. I did the demo with a messed-up voice and damaged my vocal cords even more. Now I can never really sing like I used to.

I will say God is amazing because He did not take a hardheaded kid's dream away for not listening. He just gave me another gift in music. I really don't remember all the details of how this even happened, but I wrote my first rap and got to perform it for Rob Base as he was sitting in his car waiting for his little girl. That was the turning point for me in music. He told me I had something and to put my all in. I need you to understand I never wanted to be an MC. The more people who saw and heard me rap told me I was like MC Lyte and Queen Latifah when I hit that stage. I got to work with DJ E-Z Rock, DJ for Rob Base, a couple of times. I learned a lot from them. I didn't really want to be a rapper at first, but it came to me so naturally. The more people that heard me, the better I got, and the more doors opened for me.

I am going to put you in a time machine and fast forward to the cool things. There was an audition at the Apollo Theater for the famous Amateur Night. Anyone who is trying to be in the entertainment business knows this is a big deal. My group and I were working with a couple of producers to get ready for this night. We did the audition, and the Coopers were so impressed with my group's audition they pulled us to the side. They said, "We're not going to put you in the show."

I felt so sad at that moment, but I did not show any emotion at that time. I continue to listen to them tell us what they thought of us. I was told why we were not picked for the amateur night. They wanted to take us on as their very own artist. The Coopers became our managers. We started performing at places like Harlem Week and other locations. We then got to do the Apollo as guest performers at Amateur Night with our original music and we did an amazing job. I will tell you that the Apollo stage is so big but the feeling of succeeding on a stage of greatness is overwhelming and outstanding, it's nothing like it. We knew we had something once we did well on that stage. You see, at the Apollo, it doesn't matter if you're a guest or amateur, they will boo you no matter what.

We worked with the Coopers for about a year before moving on to other people in the business. However, before we parted ways, I got to open for Full Force, The more I performed, the more it was like my calling. My first producer in the industry was Superman, Teddy Riley's DJ. We then got offered a new management contract that paid for all our needs. We had hundred-dollar shoes, beepers, and limos, picking us up to go to and from the studio it was amazing. We worked hard, spending hours rehearsing, practicing, and writing. We did so many overnights in the studio with no sleep. We started doing shows and getting paid. Our producers and managers were happy with us.

One day we were at Atlantic Records waiting to see Kevin, the A&R at the time. This was our second meeting. As I was sitting in the lobby waiting, there was this tall, slim lady with an amazing complexion. We started talking and she was really cool. She got called into the office first before me. She gave me her business card and we became friends. The person who was in the waiting room with us asked me if I knew who I was talking to. I said what do you mean. He said to read the card. I read it and the last name said Shabazz. I was like, "Okay," and the person laughed at me. I asked what was funny.

He said, "You just got Malcolm X daughter's number."

I said, "Stop playing with me."

He said, "No, that is who you were just talking to."

It was a great friendship for the time we had. I learned a lot from her about the business and what it was like to live without her dad. We never got to work together in business, but we got something better: a friendship at the time. The group and I went back to getting things together for Kevin in hopes of signing with Atlantic Records.

As things were going well, our manager had to mess it up by saying he wanted to sleep with us. How we wouldn't want for anything. He would give us a new apartment to stay in, pay all the bills, and give us spending money. What was crazy about this whole thing he was in his 50s and married. I lost so much respect for him. One day after the studio session, he told us to meet him at the office. It was like ten pm. We got there and it was a setup. He and Debbie planned to get me drugged up and sleep with me. I realized what was happening and I got out of there saying, "This will never happen." Since I didn't want to sleep with him, he broke up the group and put Debbie in a group that was getting picked up by Sony Records. Me and Debbie were no longer cool and what was crazy about this was that she and I were a couple. I walked away from the whole thing. It was as if I could not get away from men being disrespectful to women in this business. On the other hand, there are women who have no respect for themselves and will do anything to get to the top. Debbie took our manager up on his offer and started to sleep with him. I know she felt like a dumbass when Sony dropped the group overall and just went with the one girl out of four.

When you are in the entertainment business, you must deal with so much disrespect as a woman. Men will talk down to you, disregard you, steal from you, overlook you, and most of all try to sleep with you.

I would call myself the female Russell Simmons because I would act just like he did. I wouldn't let anyone get away with talking to me sideways or disrespect me at all without checking them. My name started to get around. People didn't understand how this young woman was able to navigate the way I did. I have sat in the same room with Clive Davis, MBK Records, with groups I have managed or consulted and with DJ Ron G, and Smooth from the group Nice & Smooth. That is just touching the tip of the things I have done. However, at the end of the day, where I wanted to be, was on that stage.

It felt as if I was raped all over again, but this time the perpetrators were my manager and Debbie. I didn't perform ever again as an artist. I was always the woman behind the man doing the business of my career. So, even though I stopped as an artist, and I didn't do music for a couple of years, it was not hard to come back into it, but this time it was behind the scenes. People knew I was in the entertainment game, so people would always ask me for help or input. One day, a magazine editor came to me when he saw my father and me at an event. He said to me, "I understand why you are this young, dangerous businesswoman."

I said, "Why?"

"Because I know your father and mother. Your mother was an amazing artist, and your father was a great business-minded man. It's going to be hard, but they have no idea who they are messing with when it comes to you.

I was faced again with the reputation of a woman I did not know but seemed to be a woman of greatness in this business I love so much.

Once my daughter was older, I put her in the game, hoping that things would be different with her. The older she got, the more beautiful she became. At the age of 16, she was modeling and doing fashion shows. The men were still men. They were always trying to get with my child. These men were thirty years of age trying to talk to a sixteen-year-old! Where does it stop?

I am not able to name every person I have worked with or learned from. What I want you to remember about this chapter is this: You can sit with Michael Jackson for hours, but that does not make you successful in this business. It takes hard work, determination, connection, loyalty, and most of all faith. This is a business that can be amazing from an artistic point of view.

On the other hand, there is so much corruption and secrets that would make you say there is no way in hell I would be in the entertainment business. I learned to look at it from this point of view: if all the good-hearted people who are in this business for the love and the art stop, then who will be here to help make a difference in this game? Who will keep the new generation of artists on the right side of the track? So, I stay in the game because I know my God is a great God and He will protect me and the people I help. So, if you really want to be in the entertainment game, make sure you stay educated, prayerful, and strong. Most of all, don't sell your soul.

CHAPTER 19

LGBT

Lisa

I was not sure if I was even going to talk about this. I have learned once you become a public figure from what I have been told I am becoming as well as my team. Public figures come with responsibilities. I have always taken my responsibilities, name, and my family legacy seriously. So, at many events or interviews, I have been asked did my rape turn me gay. That question at many points in my life I was not sure what the answer should be. You see, this is one other thing that I was voiceless about for so many years. I was voiceless because I didn't know myself. I started dating at the age of thirteen if you want to call it that. That was the age of my first boyfriend Jose. My next boyfriend was about the age of 14 and we dated for a couple of years, then I met Rich.

I liked boys; that was my foundation. I saw myself getting married, having kids, and being safe in the arms of a good man. That is what our role was supposed to be as women my mother/grandmother said. I didn't want to let my family down, especially my mother/grandmother and my auntie. I had questions about sexuality from time to time, but never acted on them or understood. I thought love was love.

I'm going to tell you a short story of my first confusing encounter. I am saying that because before the rape, there was a friend of mine that we were on the same team together. I was in high school. We had a game, but we stayed to see the other teams play. Her name was Sissy, she was so nice to me. We both were popular and captains on our team. On this day as we were watching the game, she sat in between my legs talking to the rest of the team. I looked at that day thinking that was not a big deal but still, I was wondering. The next game, we had Coach take us to the game. It was a small car. Sissy was like I will sit on Lisa's lap. I started to think is this something more than normal. So, we made it to the championship game. We lost the game, but it was also a very good day afterwards. Sissy and I went for a walk. As we were walking, we talked about a lot of things. Sissy's father was very strict so she couldn't do a lot of things. I understood because my family was the same way. Sissy finally told me she liked me, but it was getting late, so she asked me to call her later. We would get to school two hours early just to have time to spend together chilling with our friends. There were times when I would get into arguments that could have started into a fight, Sissy would protect me. She would either get in the person's face or pull me away from the situation. The more she and I did things like that the more it became confusing. We would meet each other in between classes all the time. I would hold her books or she would hold mine. We would walk each other to class every day. We would talk for hours on the phone. listen to music and talk about getting a place to be roommates. We had no idea what was going on between us because it was so innocent but normal to us and sometimes abnormal. I say that because we were two teenagers who liked each other but didn't understand why. If you are wondering how Sissy looked, she was shorter than me, Spanish with long, beautiful hair. I was always both tomboy and girly.

One day Sissy and I were talking, and I said, "Can I ask you something?"

She said, "You can ask me anything."

"I think I need your help."

"What can I help you with?"

"Sissy, I think I'm gay or we are gay."

She laughed at me and said, "No we not."

"Then what do you call what is happening between us? I play love songs for you, and you do the same. We talk about graduating and getting a place together."

She said, "Because we do love each other. You said you like me your dad thinks you're on the phone talking to a boy every day.

"I know, but what makes you gay? Sissy asked me.

I said, "I'm not sure. I think we are close to it."

Sissy and I came up with this crazy solution to finding out if we were gay. This solution is going to make you laugh at us—we said we would meet at lunchtime, go to one of the classrooms that was empty and kiss. If we liked the kiss, then we must be gay; if we didn't, then we were just friends.

I got to the classroom first. I was so nervous because didn't know what would happen next. Sissy finally got there and asked if I was ready and I said," if you are. We kissed, but it was ok. I couldn't say that is what we loved about each other. It didn't answer our question really. So, we just went on until her sister found out and didn't like our friendship. In our teenage years, being gay was not cool and it was not easy. They took her out of the school, and I went to another high school.

Now I need you to understand I still didn't know if I was gay or bi. Sissy was the first girl that told me she liked me, and I had feelings for her like you would a boy.

I know you must be wondering why I had to leave our school. There was a lot of people that didn't like the fact that me and Sissy had become so close. There were moments when people tried to hurt me, so the school thought It would be best to be transferred to another school for my safety.

Sissy and I had friends that was supportive. So, they helped Sissy and I see each other one more time. We said our goodbyes and said we will always love each other and never forget each other. We hugged for a long time and cried. I remember her saying they just didn't understand how wonderful you are and how great you are to me. She asked me to never change. I thanked her and she kissed me one last time. I never saw Sissy again, but I remember the love we had for each other. She was so protective of me and I enjoyed the love that Sissy showed me. We just didn't understand it.

I went on living a normal heterosexual life with no problems. I guess it was normal because I wasn't having sex with the boys I was dating. The most we did was kiss and hold hands. I worked a lot, doing speaking events and performing. Whoever I was dating then had to fit in where they could, and for the most part, they did. There were no more girls that I talked to but many tried to talk to me. I just didn't move on it because I didn't understand. Some of them who tried talking to me were cute, but I was OK.

Rich came along and I was happy, and no one had my attention but him. I didn't think about those feelings anymore that I could remember. If they did, I just overlooked them. If I go deeper, I will probably say I ignored them. Then Mike took my womanhood away and the emotion that followed was unexplainable. The visual part of men was ok, but the physical part was not what I imagined it would be anymore. I didn't desire the physical part of a man inside of me. I also wanted to be sure so I tried to get past those feelings I was missing that women should have for men. I went years trying to figure out who I was because society and religion say it's supposed to be men and women.

I also wanted to be a mother. Motherhood was very important to me. You must also know that I come from a very religious background. I love God and I didn't want to do anything that would upset Him or make Him not love me. I thank my family for teaching me about praying because I didn't want this lifestyle. I didn't want it because I was told it was wrong. I was told you would go to Hell, but I also knew who God was. I knew if I asked Him to take this away from me and change my walk if this was not for me, He would.

So, I didn't go looking for it; I didn't entertain it. I did what I was taught to do and that was to love men no matter how you were feeling. As you read this, I want you to understand that I didn't feel the amazing feeling that women feel after intimacy with men. I also need you to know that there were a lot of factors: the rape, the PTSD, the physical, and the medical. I don't think it helps having endometriosis either.

No matter how much I find men to be attractive, there are no other desires. The things I remember about intimacy with men was feeling like a piece of meat. The pain that came with intimacy. To me, intimacy with men was a job and obligation, not love.

I begged God to make me normal. I say that because back then gay was not seen as being normal. I also learned that God loves us and He will bring the right person to you. I have seen things take place that others would say wouldn't happen or shouldn't happen. If you come across a love that is natural, innocent, respectful, unconditional, kind and the person loves all of you—the good, bad, ugly and you can talk about anything, that is a love to hold on to. But the most important thing is if they love God and try to uplift you then what is there to question. Remember, the enemy wants you to think that God will not love you. The enemy wants you to feel that loving a person for who they are and not what they are is wrong. If I didn't know my God and wasn't a praying woman, I would have never loved the people I have loved.

Five years ago, a very good friend of mine who passed away due to cancer told me to make sure that I live the rest of my life being me and don't worry about what people think because God is the only person that you must answer to. She also told me that people are so quick to judge, and they are so judgmental. You can't live your life for others, you must live the life that God gave you because you are a blessing.

I am happy to say that people love me, the real me. I wish it didn't take so long to accept me. If people say they are your friends and family, they are going to love you for who you are. They just want to see you happy and loved by the right person. I am blessed to say that I had one amazing person who loved me and showed me how to love. I have to say thank you to her because she got me ready for my soul mate and the person I call my unconditional love. I also learned that true love takes time even when it's your soul mate. I must give a thank you to my big sister because on our family trip, she taught me that when you truly love someone unconditionally and they are your soul mate you can love them and still be there for them even if the timing is not now, everything is not in your time but in His time. I want you to also walk away with learning to love the person because that is all that really matters.

I'm grateful to God for the people in my life who helped me become the real authentic me. It might've taken me until my 50s to get here but I am happy that when He calls me home, I am going as the person He made me to be. So, I hope I have answered your question. PS Why would someone want a lifestyle that most of the world would judge them so harshly for if that was not who they truly were within? I do want people to walk away with an understanding that one side is not better than the other. You must get to know the person you are dating, have understanding, communication, honesty, and patience. Understand that all relationships are work, nothing in life that is worth loving and keeping comes easy all the time. You also must find a person who also loves God. If you remember these things that I am telling you, then it is possible to find that unconditional love. Please know that true unconditional love comes with no expectations. You must really understand the meaning of the words unconditional love. The love that our God gives us is truly unconditional. Here is a Scripture to refer to:

4 Love suffers long and is kind; love does not envy; love does not parade itself, is not puffed up; 5 does not behave rudely, does not seek its own, is not provoked, thinks no evil; 6 does not rejoice in iniquity, but rejoices in the truth; 7 bears all things, believes all things, hopes all things, endures all things.

8 Love never fails. But whether there are prophecies, they will fail; whether there are tongues, they will cease; whether there is knowledge, it will vanish away.

1 Corinthians 13:4-8 NKJV

CHAPTER 20

A Voice Unheard & Finally Told

Lisa & Tishaee

This was a book given to me by God to do. I didn't understand why or if I could do it. When God gave me this project, I knew it was a journey that I must do even when I didn't want to. We have told you that Olivia and I have known each other for years. I went to a play with my other bestie and saw Olivia and we reconnected. I told her about my book signing that was coming up and she told me she would come. If anyone really knows Olivia, she is a woman of her word. If she says she is going to support you, that is what she means. She came to my book signing, purchased two of my books, and helped us out the whole day. She heard me telling people my story. I told her I had neck surgery coming up; so did she. They were days apart from each other.

As friends, you check on each other. As she was recovering, she was reading the book. About a week passed, and Olivia called me and said, "I don't like you right now."

I said, "What did I do?" That is when we realized we had so much in common. We started talking about doing projects together. During that timeframe, I lost my sister and my other bestie and Olivia was right there the whole time. That was the day I knew I had three besties that I could always count on. I didn't have to explain what I was feeling or what I went through; Olivia understood. We both understood each other's past. It was easy. You see, people don't really get people like Olivia and I with a past like ours unless you've been where we have been. This book is more than just a book to us. It's about helping other people like us. We want to be the face and voice of those who are not strong enough to fight for themselves.

To add to what Lisa has stated, again this is not a project that I wanted to do; it took me a bit to jump on board, and even in this very moment, I am still on edge about this book. Lisa will tell you I stopped this journey for four months, I needed time to pray about it, do I want the world to know some of my darkness? However, I finally decided who else could explain my life better than me? No one. See so many people have and may be currently going through the same trauma I had to endure and are holding on by a thread. Please do not let that thread break. I encourage you to speak up and speak out. you are allowed to, and I promise you will eventually feel whole or semi-whole again, but you must take the first step—choose yourself first! Speak up, and don't worry about upsetting the people in the situation. The only person(s) that will be angered is your attacker(s). Do Not—I repeat—DO NOT give your abuser(s) power over your life. Let your voice be heard on the mountaintops. The new era of our time and the future is now and forever more a Voice Unheard and Finally Told.

Love you all!

Forever a P.I.A. & Nerve Wrecker but Always Uniquely Different Yet Difficulty-Unique.

Olivia Tishaee

Survivor Resources

National Sexual Assault Hotline: a service of RAINN (Rape, Abuse & Incest National Network)
Available 24 hours
Call: 800-656-HOPE (4673) English or Spanish
Chat: online.rann.org

Need to vent?
Text HOME to 741741 to connect with a volunteer crisis counselor

Department of Defense Safe Helpline Online chat hotline
Call: 877-995-5247

National Domestic Violence Hotline
Call: 800-799-SAFE

Love is Respect: a service of the National Domestic Violence Hotline
Call: 866-331-9474

VictimConnect: For all crime victims
Call: 855-4-VICTIM (84-2846)

National Human Trafficking Hotline
Call: 888-373-7888

National Center for Missing and Exploited Children
Call: 800-THE-LOST (843-5678)

Lisa Ward is a motivational speaker, published author, manager, artist developer, mentor, and founder of Avodgy Collection, Humble Doc Publishing, SECDUM Magazine, and Deadline Production/Management. Her books, Empowered by Disadvantages, & Empowered by Disadvantages Critical Thinking 2nd Edition. Chronicles her many adversities and how these have empowered and propelled her to the many successes in her life such as establishing a magazine that interviewed various famous & iconic artists. Lisa is also passionately dedicated to transforming today's youth into successful entertainers, entrepreneurs, and authors.

Ms. Ward gets her love for the entertainment industry, writing, and business hustle honestly from her birth mother and her sisters. She is the second oldest sibling of seven creative and gifted children. She has accomplished a great deal in 50-some years.

God changed Lisa's life and direction, transitioning her gifts toward impacting the youth of today. Lisa has always loved working with children and young adults. She has a strong desire to develop their careers and businesses while motivating others to view their hardships in a positive way. That is also another reason that she started a non-profit this year called "Empowered Extraordinary Voices & Artist League Inc., along with the EBD team. Keep your eyes on Lisa Ward and support her endeavors because whatever goal or project she has set her mind to, she is going to accomplish it and help as many people as she can!

***

Olivia Tishaee hails from Camden, New Jersey. As a model, wife, and mother of three, Olivia uses her character traits of being strong, loving, and hopeful to motivate others and speak life into everyone she encounters. Being a teenage mother did not stop her from achieving her goals. Mrs. Olivia is fluent in American Sign Language and is a God-fearing woman whose passion is to touch the hearts of all those who are willing to accept love and to help others in whatever way she can.

Olivia is very involved with the *Empowered by Disadvantages* mission because she understands what it is like to be part of the foster care and adoption system. Like Lisa, Olivia desires to be a voice for voiceless children; the EBD podcast and *Empowered by Disadvantages Critical Thinking 2nd edition* allowed her to accomplish this goal. Olivia positively impacts everyone that she meets. She reminds readers that you never know what someone may be going through, so please be careful about how you treat that person—you could be their last source of life. Further, we should always speak life because the tongue is a powerful weapon. Olivia chooses to use hers for good!

Special thanks go out to the sponsors of this book:

- Dr. Michael Lobis
- CJ Meenan
- Sweet Venom Effect, LLC.
- Latoya Clark
- Shana Slay Boutique
- Fashion Steppers
- Bergamot Realty, LLC.
- The LittleBigBites
- 4th District City Councilwoman Michelle Harlee
- The Beacon a collection of poems by Emerson Custis
- Jazzy Kitty Publications
- Delaware Neurosurgical Group PA
- Fashion Moment with Tai Chunn
- Ulysses Carter